LIES I TELL MY CHILDREN

Brock Macdonald

ISBN: 9781777995423

*This book is dedicated to my son Matthew who
was the inspiration for many of my columns.
I couldn't have done it without him.*

CONTENTS

Preface

Lies I Tell My Children is a collection of original Brockton's Point columns published between 1989 and 1995. Started as a concept project while in Journalism School, the columns were picked up by Shepherd Features before graduation and syndicated nationally in community newspapers across Canada coast-to-coast from Nanaimo to Goose Bay. Each of these 500 word columns is based on everday life, but with a liberal amount of creative license, as well as the use of composite characters. Many are allegorical with a point to ponder as the play on words of the column's title suggests.

Written in the early 90s, they reflect the culture, society, and technology of the times. Readers of a certain age will recognize references that may no longer be relevant. Younger readers may be at a loss wondering what a VCR is. Many are universal in their themes. But, no matter the generation, I hope you enjoy it. It's my pleasure to share the sense of humour I developed at the time as a new parent in order to cope with the situations life and my children presented. Spoiler alert, they all eventually became pretty great adults.

Jake's Your Uncle

Do you have an Uncle Jake? I've got one. They come with different names, but their attitudes are all the same. You see, Uncle Jakes all hold the unfettered belief that they are the absolute and final authority on every subject known to man. Woman too for that matter.

"What d' ya' want to be a writer for?" he asked through a mouthful of beernuts. "That's not the kind'a thing a real man does."

Yeah, like Steinbeck and that Hemingway wimp. "Gee, Uncle Jake, what do real men do?" As if I didn't know what he'd say.

"Real men work in the outdoors with tools, not sitting behind some desk tippy-tapping on a typewriter like some damned secretary or something."

It was pointless to suggest that I work outside while covering news stories and that most reasonable people, which excludes him, would consider both a 35mm camera and a computer highly technical tools. He'd just say it's not the same thing. But I'd try and run it by him. What can I say? I'm an optimist!

"It's not the same thing, boy!"

See?

"I mean real work, like excavating. There's money in that!"

Sure, if you hit oil.

"Forget writing! You can't get nothing out of it that's

worth while. Now look at me."

Well, I didn't have my wide-angle lens, but I thought I'd give it a shot.

"I only got 12 years left on the mortgage," he said, sticking his barrel chest out with pride

He's 56 years old. Pretty good, huh?

"Got me a nice set of wheels to drive."

A nine-year-old Ford club-cab pick-up the bank probably still owns.

"Only got 28 more payments."

Uh huh.

"And seasons hockey tickets."

I had him!

"Canucks seasons ticket, huh? Pretty impressive. How much does that cost you?"

"Well, when you throw in parking, food, and the beer of course . . . ."

Of course.

". . . about five grand."

"Well, I guess that's one advantage to being a writer."

"What d' ya' mean?"

"When you're a member of the press, you get to sit in the press box, high above the crowd."

"You do?"

"Sure. Best seat in the house."

"But ya' can't drink no beers up there."

"No, that's true enough," I said.

He smiled.

"That's what the media lounge is for."

The smile faded away.

"You mean there's a bar up there?"

"Sure. Bartender and everything."

"Bartender?"

"Oh, and a chef."

"CHEF!?"

"Yeah, it's great. Last time I went we had a really nice baron of beef."

"What's all that cost ya'?"

"Well, nothing, Uncle Jake."

His jaw dropped. A stunned expression seemed to suit him. It looked so natural.

"How d' ya' swing that?"

"Gee, I don't know. I guess they must pity us 'not-real-men' up there doing our 'not-real-work'."

"Smart-ass kid."

Yes, we all have our Uncle Jakes. And every time I think of him, I take a moment, close my eyes, and thank God, that I'm adopted.

Talk'n 'Bout My Generation

Remember Woodstock? It has become synonymous with the '60s and the idealistic generation who aspired to change the world. Four-hundred-thousand flower children gathered and grooved there for three days. One of them was my cousin Kenny.

"It was right on, man," he told me when he got back. I was 10. He was 22. "We became one with the universe; one within the cosmic consciousness of man."

Sounded good to me. I didn't know what the heck he was talking about, but it sounded good.

"We're gonna change things, man," he said. "When it's our turn, things'll be different. No more war, no more hate, no more greed. You wait. You'll see."

Well, it's over twenty-five years later. I don't know about you, but I haven't seen much progress in the war, hate and greed departments. In fact, I think shares in greed have split. So I decided to go see Kenny for a progress report on his promise of a better world.

I parked my eight-year-old Pontiac in front of his posh, west-side address. In the driveway sat a BMW convertible with a personalized plate, "BUY LOW". Beside it, a Jaguar XJS with the plate, "SELL HI".

I rang the doorbell and this three-piece suit answered. Looked like Kenny, sort of, but where's his hair?

"Yes?"

"Hi, Kenny."

"Do I know you?"

"Brock, your cousin. You know? We're related."

"Yes, of course. What can I do for you? Are you in the market for property?"

"Not exactly. I'm here about the world."

"I don't think that's been listed."

"No, no, no. You told me when I was 10 that your generation was going to change the world. You said when you guys got around to being in charge of things there would be no more wars, or hate, or greed. Remember?"

"Are you on some kind of medication?"

"When you got back from Woodstock you told me that your generation was going to change the world and make it a better place. Right? So where is it?"

"Where's what?"

"The better place!"

"Just a moment."

He returned a minute later with a Multiple Listing book.

"There you are. You should be able to find a nice place in there." With that he shut the door. Kenny had mutated from flower child to executroid. The world was lost and my hope with it.

Driving home I stopped for a red light in front of the old courthouse. On the steps sat a kid with green hair and a peace sign painted on his black leather jacket. Maybe hope for tomorrow lied with another generation. I rolled down the window.

"Hey, kid! Is your generation going to save the world?"

He looked at me, spat on the pavement, and said, "Save it yourself."

You know, I hadn't thought of that.

Oils Well That Ends Well

My Uncle Edison is a brilliant inventor with vision. He once predicted our civilization would have super-fast electronic ovens, small, powerful computers, and the ability to send the written word by telephone. Thing is, he predicted it yesterday.

"Nephew, come downstairs. I want to show you something."

"We are downstairs," I replied.

"Oh! So we are," he said. "All the better."

There were gadgets, gizmos, and thingamabobs everywhere. Plus a few blackened holes in the walls and ceiling.

"What happened there?" I pointed.

"Oh, just an experiment or two that didn't work out."

I made a note of the nearest exit.

"Say, Unc', what is all this stuff?"

"This isn't stuff my good lad. No, no, no. These are my inventions."

He gave me an invention of his for Christmas one year; an automatic bed maker. It turned itself on in the middle of the night and short sheeted my bed -- with me in it.

"This one for instance," he said. "You'll love this. I call it Stlitch."

"Stlitch?"

"Correct. I use it to keep things together."

"Why do you call it Stlitch?"

"Because of the sound it makes when you pull it apart." Which he did with a, 'STLITCH!'

"That's Velcro Unc."

"What?"

"Velcro! It's velcro!"

"No, it's Stlitch."

"No. Unc'. It's Velcro. Somebody beat you to it. The stuffs been around for years."

"Velcro? Velcro?! How did they get 'Velcro' from?" He pulled it again, 'STLITCH!'

"You don't get out much do you?"

He slumped into a chair. "I give up! Everything I invent either doesn't work or has been invented already. I'm nothing but a washed up old fool. I should have listened to my brother Jake and went into excavating."

"Don't be so hard on yourself." I reached across to comfort him and knocked over a can of used oil. It spread into pool of black ooze.

"Oh, scrud! Sorry, Unc'. Got any paper towels?"

"Here, use this," he said, handing me what looked like a small white pill.

"I know I can be a headache at times, but . . . ."

"No, no, no. Drop it into the oil."

"Huh?"

"Drop the pellet into the oil."

"Okay." Which I did. The oil started to disappear and the pellet began to expand. Soon the oil was gone and sitting on the counter was a brown sponge.

"What the heck is that thing?"

"Another one of my failures."

"Failures! You're kidding?"

"I had originally intended it as a bathing sponge for hotels. You know, to go with the little bars of soap they leave in your room. But, again I failed. It won't absorb water. I accidentally dropped one in some oil and consequently discovered oil is the only thing it will absorb. Now I ask you. What good is that?"

"Uncle Edison."

"Yes Nephew?"

"I think we need to have a little talk."

Acromonium

My Uncle Edison's kid Albert is one of those people who makes life more complicated for the rest of us. He's a sociologist. Way back, when life was simple, they didn't have sociologists. Now, with daily existence becoming more and more complex, they're everywhere. Hmmmm. Do we see a high, positive correlation forming here?

"Brock," he said to me, "you are SICK."

"A little eccentric perhaps," I replied, "but SICK?"

"No, no, no. By SICK I mean you fall into the category of single income, couple of kids."

"Oh, I get it. It's like yuppie," I said, "but I've never heard of that one."

"Oh there's a number of acronyms to classify people. As a matter of fact I'm doing accumulative research on the subject for my doctoral thesis."

"Really? What are some others?" I asked.

"Well, if your wife worked, you'd be a DICK."

"Did she put you up to this?"

"No, no. That stands for double income, couple of kids.

"Oh. Okay."

"But you're not a DICK, you're just SICK."

"Yes, you keep saying that."

"However, you could fall into several sub-categories of SICK which are, HICK, MICK, and LICK."

"Say what?"

"HICK is high income, couple of kids. MICK is middle

income and LICK is low income, couple of kids."

"Is there a category for not enough income, couple of kids?"

"No."

"Well, in that context, I'd much rather be a DICK."

"Now if you were a DINK . . . ."

And I assure you I'm not.

" . . . You'd be double income no kids with the subcategories being, HINK, MINK, and LINK."

"Did all of this start with yuppie back in the eighties."

"To a certain degree. But even yuppie has been broken into separate categories and sub groups."

"For example?"

"After the age of fifty a yuppie becomes a *muppie*."

"A *muppie*?"

"Middle aged urban professional."

"Oh."

"Then as they continue up the scale, they become WOOFs, or well off older folks."

"Really?"

"Unless of course they become *yuffies* before the reach the *muppie* stage."

"*Yuffies*?"

"Yes. Young urban failures."

"You're kidding?"

"No. And in that instance, they would be re-classified into another category and sub-group set."

"Like what?"

"That hinges on marital status, number of dependents and income level."

"What's the point to all of this?"

"To study humans in groups it is easier to break them down. We need to divide humans into categories that better serve the field of study. In a consumerist society the most viable system is to categorize by purchasing power and level of needs. Thus a SICK person like yourself . . . ."

I wished he'd quit saying that.

" . . . would have altogether different purchasing powers and needs from someone who's a DINK. Therefore, strong visible divisions must me made."

I don't know about you, but I think people are divided enough without Albert's help. I mean after all, why should we listen to a NITWIT -- Nutty Intellectual Twit With Imbecilic Theories.

Incommunicado

I hate cellular phones. Why? My aim in life is to pursue a slow leisurely pace. Cellular phones, by their very nature, are not conducive to that life style. Case in point. My wife and I were at an establishment of fine dining one evening. No kids, just the two of us for a nice quiet dinner. We were about to order when, BLEEP-BLEEP! BLEEP-BLEEP!. Three people grabbed for cellulars, "HELLO?", "HELLO?", "HELLO?"

Suddenly everyone was digging through attaché cases and coat pockets, "HELLO?", "HELLO?", "HELLO?". Amidst the wheels and deals that transpired that evening I decided I hated cellular phones. The week after, we went to see Silence of the Lambs. In the crucial scene, when Hannibal Lecter is about to make his escape, 'BLEEP-BLEEP! BLEEP-BLEEP!'

"No, no, no," said the guy in front of us. "It's not a bad time at all...."

I decided to wait for the video. I like VCRs. But I hate cellular phones.

I was out jogging one day when some moron in a Jaguar almost ran me over in the cross walk. The dope blew right through the stop sign with the cellular glued to the side of his head, oblivious to the fact he'd almost ended a human life, while converting T-bills to mutuals and soy bean futures. I hate cellular phones. And I knew I'd go on hating them when my little brother Bob got one. Two o'clock in the morning, the phone rang.

"Hello," I said, still half asleep.

"Hey, Brock!" said Bob. "Guess where I'm driving this morning."

"Huh."

"Into the mountains to ski. See ya'." CLICK!

I slammed down the phone and pulled the blankets over my head.

RING!

"Hello," I said again.

"Guess where I am now."

"Bob . . . ."

"On the highway about ten minutes from your exit. See ya'." CLICK!

I rolled over again.

RING!

"HELLO!" I said for the third time, now wide awake.

"Hey, Brock! Guess where I am now."

"Listen Bob . . . ."

"I'm just coming up to your exit. See ya'." CLICK!

I took the phone off the hook. I wasn't about to listen to progress reports all morning while he cruised up to the ski hi.

KNOCK, KNOCK, KNOCK.

Now what?

I opened the front door.

"Pizza."

"Huh."

"You order a pizza?"

"No! I didn't order a pizza!"

SCREECH! Bob's car came to a stop.

"Hey, Pizza dude! Over here. "Bob gave the kid a twenty. "Keep the change."

"What the heck are you doing?" I asked.

"I got hungry, so I ordered a pizza."

"You had it delivered here?"

"What was I suppose to do? Give them my license plate number and tell them to look for a red, eastbound Camaro?

I hate cellular phones.

It Came From Out'a State

With summer on the west coast comes a seasonal infestation. There is nothing you can do. Keep the doors and windows shut, take every precaution, they still swarm in. They are the most aggravating pest known to humankind; out-of-town relatives.

I suppose it's my own fault for buying a house with extra space. No sooner had I signed the mortgage than word hit the family newsletter. "EXTRA! EXTRA! BROCK BUYS HOME ON WEST COAST! SAVE THOUSANDS IN HOTEL COSTS!"

I tried to discourage their summer migration. I even had the answering machine screening calls.

"Hi, this is Brock, I can't come to the phone right now, I've got TB, the wife's in bed with diphtheria and the kids have leprosy, so I'm kind of tied up until September. Please leave your message after the beep . . . BEEP!

"Real funny, cousin," twanged the voice. "That's why I like y'all so much. We'll just sit outside 'til y'all got a free moment."

Outside? In the car? -- Y'all?

I peered through the Levelors to see a dusty Dodge Caravan with Florida plates outside.

Oh, no! Cousin Clive.

He, his wife, and their five kids waved. I waved back in resignation. I hate cellular phones.

When the seven of them filed into the living room it

was standing room only. Guess who was left standing.

"So," I said, "where're you staying?"

"Well, cousin," said Clive, "the kids can flop anywhere and the little women and I can take the spare bedroom."

Six a.m. next morning I awoke to rapping on my bedroom door.

"Huh! What! What is it? Fire? Burglar?

"Say, cousin," said Clive, "where y'all keep your grits?"

"Back east mostly." I pulled the covers over my head.

By the time I got up, the kitchen was in chaos and Clive's family was in transit.

"Well, we're off, " he said.

Thank you, Lord.

"We'll be rolling in about ten."

"Tonight?"

"What y'all making for dinner?"

"Dinner?"

"You know. Comes between lunch and midnight snack."

"Midnight snack?"

"I tell y'all, cousin, my mouth is just'a water'n for a mess'a ribs. Y'all want ribs?" he asked his family. They nodded. "Then ribs it is," and they were off.

My wife was near tears.

I picked up the phone. "Holiday Inn? I'd like accommodations for four please. Sure I'll hold."

"There's seven in Clive's family," said my wife.

"I know. The hotel room's for us."

"But they're back at ten."

"Right. We'll be gone and they'll have to leave and . . . ." Then I saw the look on her face. "Oh, no. You didn't give them a key did you?"

She hung her head in shame.

"Hello, Holiday Inn? Yes, four. And do you have a monthly rate?"

Scamarama

Have you paid your insurance bill lately? Gone up, hasn't it?

You know why don't you?

Greed.

Not just from the insurance companies. Try some of the policy holders. Policy holders like my cousin, Sam.

He called the other day. My wife answered the phone. I never do. Nobody ever calls me unless I owe them money or they want me to help them move.

"It's for you," she said. "Your cousin, Sam."

I didn't owe him any money, so I quickly thought of a medical reason why I couldn't lift anything over five pounds.

"Brock! How the heck are you?"

"Well, my back is sort of . . . "

"Grab some brewskies and come on over. I just got a wide screen TV and the Bruins are playing the Panthers on the sports channel."

"I'll be there in 20 minutes." Click.

I made it in 17 flat.

He let me into his studio apartment. I tossed him a six-pack of Miller.

Then I noticed his new TV.

"Mitsubishi 40 inch stereo with surround sound," he said. "Pretty nice, huh?"

Nice? The thing took up an entire wall. It was like

being at a drive in.

"How much?"

"Five grand."

Sam's a sales clerk at Jocks 'R Us. He gets minimum wage and 15 percent commission. To earn $5,000 he'd have to equip the entire field of the Boston Marathon.

"You're not selling drugs are you?"

"No. I was robbed."

"What?"

"Yeah. Last week. Kids I guess. They broke in and took my little black and white."

"How much was that worth?"

"I don't know. A couple of hundred bucks I guess."

"What's your deductible?"

"Two hundred."

"So how did you manage to come up with the cash for the home Cineplex."

"Don't you get it?" he asked.

"Get what?" I replied.

"I know what was stolen. And now you know what was stolen. And the thieves know what was stolen. But the insurance company don't know what was stolen."

"So in other words you . . ."

"Reported I had a little better television than I actually did."

". . . lied."

"Embellished."

"Sounds like a scam, Sam."

"You got it. Sam's scamarama."

"What did the insurance company say when you sent them the receipt for that monstrosity?"

"Nothing, dude. They just sent me a check and a form letter."

"Form letter? What did it say?"

"I don't know. Who reads form letters?"

"Let's see it," I said.

He fished around a pile of papers on the table. "Here."

I quickly read through it. "This isn't a form letter, you dope. It's a notice of policy cancellation."

"What! They can't do that?"

"Looks like you scammed yourself out of insurance coverage."

"What a bunch of crooks. They can't do that! It's dishonest!"

"Forget the beers, Sam. I'll go make some coffee."

"What for?"

"To go with your just desserts."

Phonetically Speaking

Sometimes, I wonder if my Aunt Clare is all there. I know for sure part of her is somewhere back in the sixties. Which part though, I'm certain.

Clare has a flare for the unique. Over the years she's practiced Palmistry, Tarot cards, Zen Buddhism, Numerology, Astrology, and every Hip-ology you could think of.

Now she was through practicing. Clare has taken a new direction.

"Phoneti-what?" I asked.

"Phoneticology. It deals with names," she replied.

"I thought Numerology dealt with names?" I asked.

"It does, but with mathematical values assigned to single letters of names. Phoneticology deals with the meanings of the name and how that determines ones life path."

Which space cadet came up with this one?

"I'm not surprised you've never heard of it. I've just recently developed it."

Ask a silly question.

"Would you like to hear some examples?" She asked.

"Sure." Why not?

"Well, there's Doctor Treadwell," she said.

"What does the name Treadwell have to do with medicine?"

"He's an orthopedic surgeon."

"Okay, a foot doctor named Treadwell."

"There's a couple who run a gardening center. His name is Pete Moss. Her name is Rose."

Rose Moss?

"How about a man recently cited for sexual harassment?" she said. "Do you know what his name is?"

"Lech Valwencha?"

"Max Dickoff," she said looking particularly pleased with herself

"No way!"

"Absolutely."

"Don't you think these examples are more a case of coincidence?"

"Of course they are."

Now I was confused.

"It doesn't sound like you have much faith in your new . . . in your new . . . I don't even know what to call it."

"It doesn't matter if I believe in it or not. All I have to do is make it sound feasible and there will be those who will."

"What are you trying to do, start a cult?"

"Yes, as a matter of fact, I am."

"What for?"

"Profit."

"Profit?"

"Do you know how much money people spend on religious cults and pseudo-sciences like this every year?"

"No idea."

"Tens of millions."

"Get real."

"That is exactly what I've done."

"What do you mean?"

"People want something to explain what life is all about. An answer to the big question. It's part of our nature. It's the reason why religions started. It's the reason why so-called TV evangelists like Jimmy Baker could bilk millions from the faithful. People want so much for things to make sense they let themselves be blinded by faith. They want something that puts the pieces together. Something to believe in. That's what I learned all those years I was searching."

"But Clare, what about the search for enlightenment?"

"Oh, I'm enlightened all right. I've even got nonprofit status."

Well that's Aunt Clare for you. I never figured she'd turn cynic. Yep, Clare Crook.

Hmmmm. You know, maybe there's something to this Phoneticology after all.

Zen And The Art Of Relationship Maintenance

Valentine's Day is coming and thank goodness I'm not single. Oh sure, I was once. Never again!

Developing a successful relationship is a lot of work. I know! I've spent the last 16 years working on mine. If you don't, you end up like my mechanic, Bill; with dirty hands and a broken heart.

"What's up?" I asked him.

"I'm having problems with my relationship," he said through his gloom. "You've been married forever, Brock. What's the trick?"

"The trick?"

"Yeah. How do you make a relationship work?"

Talk about being on the spot. Then I had a thought.

"Bill, you can look at relationships a lot like cars."

"Ah c'mon."

"Believe me. The two have much in common."

"How can a relationship be like a car?"

"When someone gets a new car everything about it is fresh and exiting, right?"

"Sure, I guess."

"They're always washing it and stuff, but soon the novelty wears thin and they start taking it for granted. Pretty soon little things begin to go wrong. The spark starts to fade, but it's still running, so they let it slide.

Soon everything's falling apart and before you know it, they're looking for a new ride."

"I've seen it a hundred times," he said, shaking his head.

"Well, it's the same with relationships."

"It is?"

"Sure. You've got to work on a relationship like you would a car."

"Oooh! Huh?"

"You've got to tune things up. Keep that spark alive."

"I don't get it."

"Do you change your oil?"

"Every five thousand miles."

"When's the last time you took her to live theater instead of the video store."

"Uh . . . ."

"Do you rotate your tires?"

"Yeah, sure."

"When's the last time *you* did the laundry?"

"Laundry?"

"Do you listen to the sounds your car makes?

"Sure. How else are you gonna know when it isn't working, right?"

"When's the last time you sat down and listened to her. I mean really listened about her wants, her needs -- her life?"

"Oh, well . . . ."

"What I'm saying here, Bill, is you should pay as much attention to maintaining you're relationship, as you do your car. There's no trick."

"That's it?"

"That's it."

"Well why didn't you say so in the first place?"

Sometimes, it helps to look at things in a different way. Maybe, if we all did, the roads we travel in life would be a little smoother. And if not, then we can always ride out the bumps together.

Settling Accounts

I call my wife, "The Accountant". She makes me accountable for everything.

She runs the books in our house and keeps a pretty tight reign on the finances. Buy a pack of gum, she wants a receipt. Drives me crazy! It's like living with Price Waterhouse.

It's a good thing though, I suppose. I grew up in a family without much money and never really learned how to handle it.

You should have seen me before I was married. At income-tax time, I use to dump my receipts in an envelope with a blank form and mail it to Revenue Canada with a note that said, "HERE, YOU GUYS FIGURE IT OUT."

Yes, I must admit, my wife runs our house just like a business. The way it works is at the end of every month, she gets all my receipts -- then I get the business!

"How much did you spend at the fire hall this month?" she asked.

"Let's see. Pop's a buck, and I had one, two, three, four . . . ."

"What are you going to do when you run out of fingers? Take your shoes off?"

"You count your way, I'll count mine."

"You're a writer! Write it down for crying out loud." She picked up a receipt. "Now what's this for? All it says is $1.89."

"I don't know. You said you want receipts. There's a receipt."

"There's nothing on here but a total. What am I suppose to charge this to?"

"I don't know, groceries?"

"No way, mister. I told you last month if you didn't mark the receipts, I'd charge it to your entertainment allowance."

"Oh, I remember now. It was a quart of milk. Yeah, that's it, a quart of milk."

"Too late." She opened her ledger. "Charge $1.89 to Brock."

"Have you considered a career in the Cosa Nostra, perhaps? Maybe in accounts receivables?"

"Now, where's your receipts from hockey?" she said, ignoring my comment.

"You don't get receipts playing pick-up hockey. You just fire the guy a few bucks when you get off the ice."

"Fine, then every cent unaccounted for is getting charged to you. And if you go over this month, I'll subtract it off the start of your account next month."

Like I said before, she drives me crazy at the end of every month like that. No one can pick a nit like my wife.

But I make up for it once a year.

You see, I settle the *account* on January 27. That's when she gets to see what I spent on her birthday and gets a lesson in micro-economics.

The Day After The Night Before

I suppose we've all tipped a few too many one New Year's Eve or another. Sometimes, we tip a lot too many. It's easy enough to do. Have a couple of drinks and you forget your count. Have a few more and forget how to count. Have a few more and you forget everything, until someone fills you in the next day.

That's what happened to someone I know last New Year's Eve. I won't mention any names. Let's just say she has license to nag a certain writer by virtue of marriage. Nag she has too. So it was with particular pleasure that I found her in a similar predicament.

She crawled out of bed sometime around noon to talk to Ralph on the big white porcelain telephone. After a lengthy conversation of mixed expletives and Technicolor yawns, she stumbled into the family room. "What did I drink last night?"

"I seem to remember you drinking something called a Witch Doctor at one point," I said.

"A Witch Doctor! What in heaven's name is that?"

"Rum and Diet Dr. Pepper."

"UHHGG! I hate rum."

She doesn't much like Dr. Pepper either.

"I think you just had a couple, as chasers."

"Chasers! For what?"

"The Stephen Kings."

"Stephen Kings!?"

"Pretty scary stuff, sort of like a turbo zombie."

"How many did I have?"

"Well, the final ingredient is four ounces of carrot juice . . . ."

"Carrot juice!?"

". . . And you went through a couple of quarts of the stuff."

"Oh my God!"

"I don't know why you started on them. You seemed quite happy with the Nuclear Reactors you and Aunt Sue were pounding back."

"Nuclear Reactors!?"

"Yeah, it's sort of like a Boilermaker. But instead of dropping a shot glass of bourbon in a mug of beer, you drop a tumbler of Ever Clear, into an ice cream bucket of pear cider."

"You let me do that!?"

"Hey, you're a big girl. I figured you knew what you were doing. Well, at least until the tequila."

"Tequila?"

"Yeah. You were doing shooters, but you were doing it all wrong."

"I was?"

"You're suppose to lick the salt, drink the tequila, then bite the lime. Not bite the lime, snort the salt, and throw the tequila over your shoulder."

"Oh my God."

"To quote Dorothy Parker, 'one more drink and you would've been under the host'."

"Oh my God!"

"Relax, the party was at our house."

Cruel? Maybe. I must admit, she really didn't drink that much. But I figure anyone who can't remember what they did the night before after three glasses of light wine deserves what they get.

The Complexities Of Love

Relationships can be a perplexing experience for those uninitiated to finer points of romance. Take, Danny, one of the rookies at my volunteer fire hall. He was having a devil of a time figuring out what to get his girl for her birthday. Lucky for him there were two old pros around to ask, like my buddy Chester and me.

We were upstairs shooting a game of pool when Danny walked in with a befuddled look on his face. "Can you guys give me some advice?"

"Advice?" I asked. "What kind of advice?"

"I've been going out with this girl for a couple of months now and I don't know what to get her for her birthday."

"Oh, is that all!" I said. "That should be pretty easy."

"Not so fast," said Chester. "This could be a turning point in the relationship. You want to make sure you get the right gift."

"That's what I'm afraid of," replied Danny. "I was just going to buy her some chocolates."

"Is she overweight?" asked Chester.

"Well, she's not fat or anything, but she could stand to lose a couple of pounds."

"Never buy an overweight person chocolates," said Chester. "If she's like most people with a few extra pounds she's probably dieting. If you give her chocolates, she'll feel compelled to eat them. She'll throw her diet off, gain back any weight she's lost, Then blame you because you gave them to her."

"Oh Jeez," said Danny.

"On the other hand," offered Chester, "if you don't give her chocolates she might think you think she's fat and she'll be insulted."

"Oh Jeez," said Danny.

"How about jewelry?" I offered. "That's a pretty safe gift.

"Yeah, I thought about that too," said Danny.

"You have to be careful with that though," said Chester. "If you give her cheap jewelry, she could equate that with the value you put on the relationship and she'll think you don't care enough about her."

"Oh, right," he said.

"Of course," said Chester, "if you give her expensive jewelry it could send her a very different message. She might think you're trying to buy her affections and she'll really feel insulted."

"Oh Jeez!" said Danny.

"Why don't you just buy her some flowers," I said, "maybe a dozen long stemmed roses or carnations?"

"Yeah, I could do that!"

"Does she have allergies?" asked Chester.

"Uh, gosh, I don't know," replied Danny.

"The last thing you want to do is give a person with allergies flowers," said Chester. "They'll start wheezing, and sneezing, and feel like mud by the time the nights over."

"Oh Jeez," said Danny, shaking his head. "Well, thanks, guys." He turned and headed down the stairs.

"You figure out what you're going to do?" I asked.

"Yeah. I'm just going to call her up and break it off. Thanks again for your advice." He clumped off down the stairs.

"Anytime," Chester called after him. "Glad we could help."

"So, Chester," I said, "how's the divorce coming along?"

"Not bad. Why?"

A Toast With Jam

Right about now you've probably got a wedding invitation or two. Some of you are even going to have to get up and say a few words. You may even be asked to make the toast to the bride.

We've all heard one of those traditional little numbers before. Someone gets up, says what a great girl Mabel is, tells an embarrassing anecdote from when she was 12, comments on what a lovely woman she grew up to be, then down the hatch. How boring and unfair.

I mean after all, research indicates 50 percent of those who get married are men. (You thought I wouldn't check, right?) They've got just as much right to be humiliated as anyone else.

So why not have someone give a toast to the couple? Start a new trend. If you did, it could sound something like this.

"I've been asked to say a few choice words here today, and since my wife is in attendance, I guarantee you I will choose very carefully, because the subject of my little talk is -- marriage.

There's a lot to be said about marriage, but who's got the time or the nerve?

This marriage thing usually happens after two people fall in love. Sounds romantic, doesn't it? They say love is blind and the only cure for love is the institution of marriage. I must conclude, therefore, that marriage is an institution for the blind.

Some say that 'happily married' is a contradiction in terms.

On the other hand, you never know what happiness is until you get married -- unfortunately by that time it's too late.

Sometime after we get married, usually right after the honeymoon, we wonder if we've made the right choice.

After all, no woman ever falls in love with a man unless she has a better opinion of him than he deserves.

And the reason he thought she was an angel, he discovers, is because she's always up in the air harping on something.

Marriage is many things.

It is like getting into the bath, which everyone knows, once you get used to it it's not so hot.

It is like a three a.m. phone call. There's a ring, then you wake up.

There are many things marriage is not.

It is not a 50--50 proposition. Anyone who thinks it is doesn't know anything about relationships or fractions.

Nor is it a state based of equality. The only time a husband and wife see eye-to-eye is if they happen to be the same height.

And while brides seem to have an intuitive way of handling their new husbands. The grooms are not so fortunate. After all, there are only two ways to handle a woman -- and nobody knows either of them. So have a happy life together and always remember, a successful marriage is falling in love again and again and again. And it really helps if it's with the same person.

Here's Rice In Your Eye

My wife and I were the first to get married in our crowd. Since my in-laws were picking up the tab, I invited everybody I knew, making it obligatory to invite me to their weddings. This, of course would provide me with evenings of free food and drink for years to come. Consequently, I've seen lots of weddings and I've seen what works and what doesn't work. So here's some do's and don'ts for soon-to-be brides and grooms.

A don't: Never have a best man who's better looking than you. Most people at weddings don't know the groom from the Zamboni driver. Everyone will mistake him for you and stuff envelopes of cash in his hand and then try to set you up with the cousins with the great personalities. Which, if you'll remember, is how you got in this predicament in the first place.

A do: Always remember to thank the new in-laws for giving you such a lovely, kind, intelligent woman for your life partner. This always scores big points and lays the seed for when you hit them up to finance your first house.

A do: When people start clinking their glasses to make you kiss, make the table that started it stand up and sing a song. Why should you be the only people humiliated during the evening?

A do: Always place an armed guard on your getaway car. I knew one couple who had theirs encased in rubber cement with a note that said, "Now you can practice safe sex in the car."

A don't: Never arrange for your Uncle Artie, who your dad and the rest of the guys at the fire hall think is so funny, to be the emcee. Why? Well the reason they think he's funny is because of the off-color jokes he tells. The last thing you need is some dope in a polyester suit starting off the evening with, "There was these three hookers, see and uh . . . ."

A do: Always make fun of the out of town guests. That way you get their gifts, but you won't get an invitation to their wedding, thus saving you enormous travel costs.

Well that's about it, except for one more thing about gifts. Remember to save the receipts, because it's not what you get, but how much you can get for it when you take it back that counts.

Irreconcilable Differences

When you're married, you start to develop couples as friends. It's just the way things work.

But the way things work, couples you like, won't like each other.

We're fortunate with the couples we have as friends. There are only two who don't get along. Not to worry, they more than make up for the ones who do.

The first time they got together the hostilities began.

It was a regular Saturday night; the boys downstairs watching hockey, the girls upstairs complaining about the guys being downstairs watching hockey. It was the regular drill. What could happen?

What happened first was a Penguins-Red Wings game. And as luck would have it, bad luck that is, one guy was a Pittsburgh fan, the other was gung-ho for Detroit.

What started as a debate about who's the best player, Lemieux or Yzerman -- (a mute point since anyone who knows anything knows Cam Neely is the greatest hockey player that's ever lived) -- soon turned into a donnybrook.

I started upstairs to fire on a black and white striped shirt and restore some order, when I met my wife on her way down.

"How's it going?" I asked.

"Not good."

"Why? What's up?"

"Sue tried to sell Donna some Mary Kay cosmetics."

"What's wrong with that?"

"Donna's an Avon Lady."

I knew then there could be no reconciliation.

We barely got through dinner, then went on to the games.

First we tried hearts. But every chance she had, Donna gave Sue the *Bitch.*

Then we tried trivial pursuit. Half way through the game we figured out why Donna hadn't gotten any right. Sue was making up the questions.

I started making excuses to leave, unfortunately it was my house. Finally they got the hint and left.

About a month later I came home to find my wife having coffee with Sue, who was full stride in a diatribe.

"How did you ever meet people like that, Terri?" she asked. "I mean Donna is about as dry as unbuttered popcorn. And her Husband, what's-his-name, has the personality of a bald tire. And Stupid! My Lord! How long did it take her to realize I was making up those questions in trivia? I wasn't cheating or anything, I thought she'd clue in after the first one. But it went on and on and on . . . . Oh, Brock! Goodness you must think me awful. I come over for coffee and here I sit cutting two of your best friends down like this, shame on me."

"That's okay," I said. "You should hear how they talk about you when we're with them."

A Tangled Web

My friend Chester has two things in common with Felix Unger. He was asked to remove himself from his place of residence, and that request came from his wife.

So, I did what a best friend is supposed to do. I took him out to hear his tale of woe, and buy him a beer. She'd cleaned out the joint account.

"I don't get it," he said. "I provided a good income, I did my share of the childcare and domestic chores. I was supportive and sensitive to her needs. Where'd I go wrong?"

I knew one guy who's wife, during their divorce, accused him of sexually abusing their children. She dropped the accusation after he agreed to give her the house and pay her legal fees.

Two women sat down in the booth next to us.

"We're not going to Hawaii with the Rimsteads now," said the first one.

"Really?" said the second, unenthusiastically.

"No, we're taking our regular holiday in Las Vegas. But we have to put it off until September. George can't golf in the heat. It really doesn't matter to me when we go because the casinos are air conditioned. I never see daylight until we're on the plane home. But he's got a lot of nerve making me wait."

"Does this mean you're staying together?"

"Not on your life! I'm going to have him served with the papers and a restraining order the Friday before

Christmas."

"You're kidding?"

"He won't even be able to find a lawyer until the new year. When I'm finished with him in court, he'll be lucky if he has enough left for the parking meter. And the piéce de résistance will be when I get that damned sailboat of his."

"His sailboat? Didn't he inherited that from his father."

"So? I'll demand the children and negotiate everything he owns for joint custody. I'll have the house, the best of his portfolio, and his damned boat! Then I'll stick him with the kids, sell that oversized bathtub toy, and buy a condo in Maui. And if the kids want to visit, he can pay their airfare."

The waitress brought their drinks.

"I've got it," said the first one.

"No, no. Don't be silly," said the second.

"Silly nothing! I've got George's American Express. Say, why don't you leave Harold? You could live near me in Maui."

"Why would I want to leave Harold? I love him."

"Love! What does love have to do with anything?"

Chester and I hadn't said a word, but we knew we were thinking the same thing -- poor George.

"Does the words nut and buster come to mind?" asked Chester under his breath.

"Yeah," I said, "and some eat their young too, apparently."

With that, Chester jumped up.

"Hey! Where are you going?" I asked.

"Pay phone," he replied.

"What for?"

"To check on the kids."

The Best Things In Life Are Free

I had a bet with my wife to see who could provide the best evening of entertainment for the lowest cost. The loser had to get up with the kids every weekend for a month.

It was writer versus accountant and I was up against the cheapest bean counter since flints were skinned.

She won the toss (kept it too), chose to go first, and cheated right off the bat. I got dinner at home and a video. Whoop dee doo!

"Total cost, twenty five dollars and thirteen cents. Beat that Mr. Saturday morning cartoons."

No problem.

You see, I was writing a business article about a prominent local restaurateur. As part of the research, he invited me to be his guest for dinner at his newest five-star restaurant called, Seasons On The Hill. It's built on an old rock quarry on the highest ground in town. The only place with a better view is a passing 747. I couldn't lose if I tried.

She looked at the menu. "The prices aren't bad for the venue, but there's no way you're going to beat me on this."

"You order anything you want."

"Then you concede?"

"Certainly not."

"You're not planning to eat and run are you?"

"Certainly not."

So we ordered with reckless abandon and proceeded to enjoy the best prepared and served meal either one of us could ever remember. The chef even paid us a visit with a little tidbit of his newest creation.

After our coffees, our waiter came by and said, "I hope you've had a pleasant evening, Mr. Macdonald. Everything has been taken care of."

"Thanks, Mark," I said. "It was superb."

"What's been taken care of?" whispered my wife.

"The check."

"What did you do? Threaten to yell, Rat?"

"I know the owner. Dinner was on him," I replied, as I put a twenty onto the table for Mark.

She walked out to the car in silence as the fact she might lose sunk in.

"You still have to provide after-dinner entertainment," she said, as I drove down the hill to Nat Bailey Stadium, where the local triple A team was in the top of the seventh. We parked on the street, walked into the ball park past the unmanned turnstiles, found empty seats in the stands, and ordered two brewskies from a vender.

I paid the five dollars and turned to my wife. "That brings my total to twenty five dollars even. You'll have to admit, I won."

After the game we headed for the car and saw the cop just as he pulled away. I ran up and snatched the ticket from the window. "TWENTY FIVE DOLLARS!"

"Ha! You're over budget now, pal," said my wife, gloating. "You lose!"

I couldn't believe it. I had everything planned so well. Then it hit me.

"Lose? I think not."

"What about the ticket?"

"It doesn't add to my total."

"And why not? It's your ticket."

"You're right," I said, as I handed it to her, "But it's your car."

School Daze

I went to five high schools while I was growing up. When class reunions rolled around, I couldn't decide which one to go to, so I didn't go to any.

That's not exactly true. I did go to one. My wife's. She went to a school I somehow missed.

They gave me a blank name tag at the door. Nobody knew me, so I wrote, Terri's Husband.

Terri had already connected with some old friends, so I wandered over to get a cold one.

Suddenly, there's this guy in my face. "It's me! Charlie!" He looked at the nameplate. "Terry Husband, right?"

"Well . . . ."

"So what are you doing now?"

"What was I doing before?"

"Ha, ha, you haven't changed a bit. Well, besides the weight."

Why I ought'a . . . .

"Hey, look over there, it's the Gizmo."

"The Gizmo?" I asked.

"Yeah, remember? Glasses, pocket protector, calculator, first guy on the block to own a pong game."

"Yeah, I remember." Every high school I went to had one.

"Hey, Giz!"

The Giz wandered over.

"Remember me?" asked Charlie.

"Do I have a choice?" replied Gizmo. He looked at me. "You've put on weight haven't you?"

What is this?

"So what are you up to now, Giz?" asked Charlie.

"Software."

"Sales or service?"

"Concept, design and mass production."

"Well, excuse me, Mr. Gates. Hey, look! There's Pete and Slider," said my new old-acquaintance, "and Slider's still wearing Dayton boots."

They joined us, one in leathers and Levi's the other in sweats and Nikes.

Slider punched Gizmo lightly on the arm. "Hey, Gizmo, what's the square root of Wanda Lavalee's vital statistics?"

"Nine point eight nine nine four nine three," replied Gizmo.

They all laughed.

"Still got your bike, Slider?" asked Charlie.

"Not anymore. Kind 'a hard to put a car seat on the back."

"Got married, huh?"

"Yeah, to Wanda Lavalee." They laughed again.

So there I sat all evening with the class clown, the nerd, the greaser, and the jock, as if we were friends all our lives. Around midnight my wife came to drag me home. They all waved and jeered as I followed her outside.

"Did you know those guys?" she asked.

"Yeah, sure. We went to different high schools together."

Through The Ages

My Walkman blaring Green Day, I bounced around the family room pulling riffs on my air guitar. Just when I was about to cut into a wild guitar solo in Basketcase, I looked up. There stood my wife, arms folded and mouth in motion.

I lifted one side of my head set. "Say what?"

"Do you know how ridiculous you look?" she asked.

"Is this a trick question?" I replied.

"Grow up and act your age!"

Hmmmm. How do you act thirty-five? Is there an acceptable group and an unacceptable group of behaviors for people in their thirties? Air guitar's out, but bungy jumping's okay?

I reflected one of the first times someone questioned the age appropriateness of my behavior. I was almost four, had an owied knee and was screaming my head off. A big person finally came along. "Oh relief," I thought.

But instead of picking me up to offer comfort, they bent down and said, "Come on, act your age!"

Like a three-year-old is going to say, "Okay, dude, just give me a shot of bourbon and a bullet to bite on while you sew up this gaping hole. Yeah, just stick the kneecap back in. That's right, I can take it."

Then, there was first grade. One day I grabbed my fathers lunch by mistake. Upon the first bite I discovered green onions in the egg salad sandwich. Green onions are like kryptonite to little kids. Consumption was out of the question.

My teacher, Miss Attila, felt my revulsion for onions was a breach of her authority and my verdant complexion a blatant attention seeking antic. So, she promptly marched me down to the office and proceeded to give me the strap.

WACK! "You vill learn," WACK! "to behave," WACK! "like za proper young man!" WACK! "and act your age! Yah?" WACK! WACK! WACK!

When we returned, Peggy Grutenvelt had eaten my lunch, thus saving me the further embarrassment of having it shoved down my throat. I could have kissed her, except girls at that point, were double kryptonite.

My attitude towards women changed near the end of grade seven. I figured it was time to pay Peggy back for her lunch rescue maneuver. But my affectionate attempt to square things only got me a right cross square in the jaw.

"You're so immature," she said, when I regained consciousness. "Grow up and act your age?"

The same darn thing my wife had just said. So I turned my Walkman off and said, "Okay, would you care to suggest something more suitable for someone of my advanced years? After all, you've been there a lot longer than I have."

I turned Green Day back on, drowning out the verbal tirade my wife was delivering on my otherwise occupied ears.

Hey, I may not act my age, but at least I admit to it.

"Do you have the time, to listen to me whine . . . ."

Labor Pains

Witnessing your child's birth is something I recommend to all prospective fathers.

However, it behooves me to make another recommendation. Skip the labor part.

Why?

Well, in my father's day, men would pace the waiting room smoking cigarettes until a nurse brought the happy news.

Those days are gone.

Now men spend months in pre-natal classes learning to help their partners and take an active role in the birthing process, which is good.

However, while you're taught to be more supportive, no one tells you about the personality change the soon-to-be mom goes through.

Quite frankly, I'll never be able to look at a pregnant woman again without the phrase 'Attila the Mum' coming to mind.

Now, I know birth is a painful thing for a woman. I'm told there's nothing a man can experience that would even come close. And for that, I'm truly grateful.

My wife was in labor for 36 hours with our first child. I was there by her side. And I've got the x-rays of the broken bones in my hand to prove it.

On the day labor began, I dropped my wife at the maternity ward, then returned home for the all the stuff we remembered to pack, but forgot to bring.

When I returned to her room, one bed was empty and a curtain was around the other.

"I'm back," I announced.

"This is all your fault you son of a $@*&!," cursed the voice behind the curtain.

"Who? Me?"

"Yes you, you *&%#! You're never laying another hand on me again. EVER!"

"I don't think hands were the problem. Did you skip guidance class in high school?"

"I can't do this. Forget it. I'm going home, I'll come back tomorrow. GO GET THE CAR!"

"I really don't think that's a good idea."

"YOU got me into this position you $#%&*! NOW YOU GET ME OUT!"

A nurse came in. "Can I get you anything, dear?"

"YES!" shrieked the voice behind the curtain. "A CE-SAREAN FOR ME, AND A VASECTOMY FOR HIM!"

The nurse chuckled and walked away. "Very amusing, Mrs. Ferguson."

"Mrs. Ferguson?" I pulled open the curtain.

"You're not my #%&* husband!" screamed a very pregnant stranger.

Just then my wife waddled through the door.

"Oh, there you are," I said.

"WHAT YOU DOING OVER THERE YOU ROTTEN SON OF A &*@#$?"

"OH, just getting a little practice in."

Out Of The Mouths
Of Babes

Having married friends who don't have children can be a great advantage for those of us who do.

I don't mean couples who haven't started families yet. They're too busy savoring the last precious moments of freedom.

I mean the couples who have chosen not to have children.

Every once in a while the notion strikes them that they must be missing something. They'll see their friends who have kids and before you know it the yearning starts.

When that time comes the couple turn to friends, like my wife and I, who have a small supply of the little darlings, and offer to rent one for the weekend, so they can see what they're missing. Or aren't missing as the case may be.

It's kind of nice, we get a break, the kid gets spoiled rotten, and the childless couple gets to reinforce the correctness of their conviction to remain childless.

But to me, an added benefit is hearing how the weekend went from the returning offspring. Five-year-olds are so honest. What I like best is how they tell the story. Especially when they use new words and phrases they've picked up over the weekend. There's no telling what the little dears will do to the English language.

"So, Krissy, what did you do at Aunt Patty's?"

"First we went to see a moodie."

"A Moodie?"

"At a theater near you."

"Oh, okay. Which one?"

"Addalin."

"Really? Sounds like a headache remedy."

"Nope. That's tryanoll."

"Okay. Then what did you do?"

"We went back to Auntie Patty's and played games on the pomcuter and then we watched Gigglelin's Island."

"Gigglelin's Island?"

"He's a raiding lunartic. Aunt Patty said so."

"I see. Then what?"

"Then we had a manromic dinner."

"A what?"

"A manromic dinner. With candles on the table. Aunt Patty let me light them."

"And what did you have for dinner?"

"We had real cutless."

"Real cutless, huh? Not synthetic cutless?"

"Nope, real cutless."

"What else?"

"Fetchagenie afraido."

"Afraido?"

"It was green."

"Yum."

"And I got to have pop and milk."

"At the same time?"

"Mixed together."

"Uh, huh."

"Aunt Patty had wine. That's booze, it's got alcohol. I told her if she drank too much she'd have to go to Schick, where they'll help her lose the cravings."

"What did Aunt Patty say about that?"

"Nothing. She got something stuck in her throat and Uncle Larry had to grab her around the tummy and give her a hemlock manure."

"A hemlock manure, huh?"

"Yep."

"Did Aunt Patty say when she was going to have you over again?"

"Yep. And I can hardly wait. I've never seen a blue moon before."

Lies I Tell My Children

My parents lied to me. You know what I'm talking about. They told little lies to explain things too complicated or sensitive for me to understand at a young age.

They were pretty lackluster lies though.

The three-miles-to-school-in-the-snow bit was particularly lame. Considering I walked over two miles in snow to school myself, the old boy's extra half mile didn't seem like much of a hardship -- barefoot or not!

If you're going to lie to your kids, why not have some fun? Be creative. They'll figure out the truth eventually anyway, right? What's the harm?

Kids' standard questions and parents' standard answers go something like this.

STANDARD QUESTION: "Can I have some licorice?"

STANDARD ANSWER: "No. You'll spoil your dinner."

Boring!

So I say.

"Sorry, but today's a Tuesday. And local bylaw RBS 386 states no licorice shall be purchased for consumption on a Tuesday, unless it's the fifth Tuesday of a month with a R in it during a leap year."

It works for me.

How about Christmas lies?

STANDARD QUESTION.

"Daddy, how does Santa know if I've been naughty or nice?"

STANDARD ANSWER.

"Because he's magic, honey."

He's magic? I never ever believed that one.

But what about appealing to the paranoia in all of us?

"Because he has undercover elves who have infiltrated every facet of our society disguised as dentist's receptionist, school secretaries, cashiers, bus drivers, even little kids. They're all computer linked to the north pole by a vast, satellite network, so you better be good for goodness sake."

I love that one. It even works in the summer.

How about giving a kid a reason after saying: "DON'T JUMP ON THE BED!"

STANDARD QUESTION: "But why not, it's fun?"

STANDARD RESPONSE.

"Because you fall down and break your neck."

Sorry, not enough of a threat.

So I say, "Because when you jump on the bed it wakes up the monsters who live underground. And every jump brings their elevator higher and higher until finally, they're right up to the trap door where they hide under your bed until you're asleep. Then they sneak out in the middle of the night and eat your face."

How about this classic?

STANDARD QUESTION: "Daddy, where do babies come from?"

STANDARD ANSWER: "Go ask your mother."

What a cop out. I don't think kids should be lied to about something as important as this, do you? So at this point I tell them the truth. I mean after, all my parents were honest with me on this one.

"Well, honey, there's this place called Babylonia where vast cabbage patches grow in amongst these stork nest, see? And . . . ."

Old Fashioned Fairy Tales

There are some great books around for kids these days. Books that teach valuable lessons to develop strong principles, sound reasoning, and clear thinking.

All I had when I was a kid were the old standbys: Cinderella; Jack and the Beanstalk; Goldilocks.

My kids have heard a version or two of them. But after being exposed to the new children's literature, kids find some definite problems with those old stories.

". . . Goldilocks woke up, saw the three Bears, and ran home never to venture into the forest again." I closed the book.

"Did she get arrested, Dad?"

"Excuse me?"

"Did Goldilocks get arrested?"

"For what?"

"Daaaaad! She went into the Bears' house when they weren't home, broke Baby Bear's chair, and ate their food."

"Essentially correct, but . . . ."

"What if the Bears hadn't come home. She might have stole stuff."

"Have you been watching America's Most Wanted again?"

"They should have called the police."

"I don't think bears have phones."

"They had a stove to cook porridge."

Good point.

It got worse with Jack and the Beanstalk.

". . . Jack chopped down the beanstalk and the giant came tumbling down. Jack took the goose that laid golden eggs to his mother and they lived happily ever after."

"What happened to the Giant?"

"Got killed I guess."

"Hold on a minute! Jack killed the giant? He should go to jail."

"What for?"

"Daaaaad! Let's get this straight. First Jack broke into the Giant's castle. Right?"

"Yes," I admitted under cross examination.

"Then, stole the goose. Right?"

"Well, yes. But . . . ."

"Then killed the Giant. Right?"

"Well, yes. But . . . ."

"But nothing, Dad! That's a class A felony. Jack should get life. Don't you know any stories about good people?"

Then there was Cinderella.

". . . the Prince and Cinderella lived happily ever after."

"What about the step mother?"

"What about her?"

"I think Cinderella should have got a lawyer and sued her."

"Sued her!? For What?"

"She was mean. She made Cinderella do all the house-work. I think that's child abuse."

"I don't think they had lawyers then."

"Sure they did, Dad. Everyone knows lawyers are the oldest profession.

Kids And College

It's tough going to college when you've got kids. Take last Saturday morning. The sun's shining and everyone's still in bed except me and the four-year-old who's glued to the box watching Pee Wee's Playhouse. A perfect time to get some of the reading done on my optional list of thirty-odd, six-inch-thick, hardcovers that contain maybe a page or two of useful information.

One title was recently named by the Library Technicians Association as the edition most likely to herniate. Another was chosen as the best book to be stranded on a desert island with. It takes you twenty years to read the darn thing, then you can start over because you'll have forgotten what was at the beginning.

And when you're not reading you can bench press it to stay in shape.

Well, no sooner had I reached for my book when my four-year-old's attention immediately shifted from Pee Wee and the Playhouse Gang to me. It's an autonomic reflex that all small children have. As soon as they detect their parents attention diverting from them to something that's really important something called an annoydil gland kicks in and fills their tiny brains with a hormone called interferelin.

It doesn't matter what you're trying to do, they will find a way to keep you from doing it.

"Daddy."

"Yes, dear?"

"What are you going to do with me today?"

"Well, nothing actually. I was planning on getting some of my reading done."

"Don't you want to play with me?" she asked, batting those big eyes that can inflict a feeling of guilt so intense you expect a social worker to show up at your door and accuse you of neglect.

An attempt to get you on an emotional level like that you can live with. When they try to exert themselves intellectually is when the real trouble starts.

Children's logic is very complicated, not only is it based on incomplete information, but they also make it up as they go along. And if you want to win an argument with one, you have to relate it to something they can understand. Such as material greed, which is an innate quality of the North American child. They may not be born with a silver spoon in their mouths but they all want a BMW in the Fisher Price garage.

"Look, honey. If I don't get my homework done I won't pass the course. If I don't pass the course I won't graduate. If I don't graduate I can't get a job. And if I can't get a job we'll have no money and the bank will take our house away and we'll lose everything we own and we'll have to live in an alley in a cardboard box and eat dog food."

"Dog food? Yuck! What does that taste like?"

"Have you ever eaten in a college cafeteria?"

"Nope."

"Then it might be a little hard to explain." Then it came. The one utterance that parents fear the most.

"Why?"

That was it she had me. It was the dreaded "why". It wouldn't matter what I said at that point. Everything could be countered with a, "why".

"Because college food has to be experienced to be fully appreciated."

"Why?"

"Because college food sucks."

"Why?"

"Because it's synthetic."

"Why?" I capitulated.

"All right, Krissy. Get the crayons." Oh, well. Maybe when she's not looking I can color an essay or something.

Who Put The Birth In Birthday, Anyway?

Do you consider yourself a selfish person? Of course not. Who does, right?

But when it comes to birthdays, selfish is exactly what we are. We expect cake, we expect gifts, and we expect to be the center of attention because over the years that's what we've come to, well, expect.

But my littlest kid, the boy, saw things differently on his third birthday. He was at that funny age; old enough to understand something called a birthday was happening, but not old enough to have those self indulgent expectations.

I thought he was a little confused still, so I took him to the mall for a malt to explain things.

"You know what today is, little guy?"

"No, fargy."

Fargy is his favorite word. I'm not sure what it means, but everything to him is a fargy.

"Today is your birthday."

"CAKE!" he shouted kicking his feet.

"Yeah, cake's part of it, but that's not what it's all about. Today's the day you were born."

A quizzical look grew on his face. Born wasn't in his vocabulary yet. Too technical. I tried a different approach.

"How old you are now, Matt?"

"Thrweee!" he shouted.

"Right! Three years ago today, daddy took mommy to the hospital and Dr. Lee took you out of mommy's tummy."

That got his attention. He looked at his stomach, then back at me with his head cocked. "Nope," he said, head shaking as he went back to work on his malt.

"Yep," I said.

"Nope."

"Really, that's where little kids come from. Their mommy's tummy."

He shot me that look again.

"Here's what happened," I said. "You grew in mommy's tummy for 9 months. When you were ready to be born, mommy started to get tummy aches. That's when Dr. Lee took you out of mommy's tummy."

"Di't hurt mommy?"

"Well, yeah it did. But that's the way it works. Do you understand now?"

"Yep," he said, draining the last of his malt"

"So, what do you want for a birthday present."

"Mommy fargy!"

"You've already got a fargy . . . I mean a mommy."

"No! Mommy present!"

"What's that? You want to give your mom a present?"

"Yep."

"It's your birthday, kid."

"She borned me."

I sat for a moment and let what he said sink in. He wanted to give his mother a present on his birthday because she had given him the greatest gift of all, life.

We went to Hallmark and made one of those custom greeting cards. I helped him with the wording, trying keep it in the spirit he meant, and without using fargy. When we were done, it read, *"Mom, thanks for my birthday! I not sure what it meant to you, but it was everything to me."*

We went home and he gave it his mother.

"Thanks, Matthew. What a nice boy," she said, giving him a big hug.

He pushed away from her and yelled, "Fargy Cake! Where's my fargy cake?"

Ah, yes. They learn so quickly, don't they?

It Slices, It Dices, It Ties Its Own Shoes

"My Uncle Walt is a recluse. He's lived up country by himself all his life and really doesn't like being around people. Especially little people.

We manage to coax him out of his house once a year, for the family get together on New Years Eve, with the threat that if he doesn't show, we'll visit him -- often.

It works every time.

He's not a bad old guy.

You see, he doesn't see a need for anything that hasn't got a useful purpose. Well, useful to him anyway. And Uncle Walt doesn't see anything useful about little kids.

"Don't you ever wished you married and had kids Uncle Walt?"

"What for? I got no need for a wife. I got no need for Little'ns either. All they ever do is get under foot."

"Well kids have their uses you know."

"Like what?" he asked, shifting in his chair.

"Paper fetcher."

"Paper fetcher?"

"Yeah. This is a good one, especially if you don't have a dog. You pour your morning coffee and seconds later there's the kid with the paper."

"I got a dog."

"Oh, yeah. I forgot."

Ugly one too.

"Well, have you got a TV?" I asked.

"Yeah."

"Back-up remote control."

"A what?"

"Sure. When the battery runs down in the remote control they can change channels. Just hold up a flash card with the number of the channel you want and let them match it."

"Flash cards!"

"No kidding. You can use the flash cards for lots of other things too."

"Like what?"

"To use your little kid as an automatic phone dialer."

"Automatic phone dialer?"

"They can dial the numbers you show them with the cards. And when they learn the numbers you can convert them into a voice activated phone dialer. Pretty high tech huh?"

"High what?"

"Do you ever get those annoying phone calls from carpet cleaning companies?"

"Yeah, I ain't got any carpets. Takes ten minutes just to tell'm."

"Here's where a little kid can really come in handy."

"How's that?"

"As an anti-telephone-solicitor device."

"Anti-telephone what?"

"Anti-telephone-solicitor device."

"How's that work?"

"When you get one of those annoying calls just hand the phone to the little kid. They'll talk to anyone. You won't get return calls and you'd be surprised how much their vocabulary improves."

"I'll bet." He smiled.

For a second, I thought his face was going to crack.

Just then my little girl appeared and handed him a glass of eggnog.

"Here, Uncle Walt," she said, looking around to make sure no one else could hear.

"And I made mommy put some rum in it too."

He smiled again.

"Are you trying to get on my good side little girl?"

She put her hand to her mouth and giggled.

"Silly, you don't have a bad side." She hugged him and ran off.

He smiled at me and said, "Boy, did you put her up to that?"

"Not me," I replied. "She's been on automatic for months.

Vinnie The Shmoozer

Ever buy a used car?

One day I spotted a hot-looking Daytona Turbo Z. I wanted it. I wanted it bad.

I don't usually deal with car lots, but this was an upscale, German dealership. I figured if anyone would be straight, it would be these guys.

Silly me.

I walked up to the first person I saw. He was a little guy, with a pencil thin mustache. His shifty eyes that seemed to take in everything.

"Are you . . . ?"

"The sales manager? Yep, Vinnie Testarosa."

"I'm here about the . . ."

"Job?"

"Well . . ."

"Say. You ever shmooze cars before, kid?"

"Shmooze?"

"Sell, sell."

"Well . . . ."

"Not a lot of experience, huh, Kid? That's okay. I'm gonna show you how to shmooze. Pick any car on the lot."

"How about that black Daytona"

"Perfect. Kid, you're gonna love this." He walked quickly, hands continually in motion, "Let's say you're a customer."

"Okay." I said. That was pretty easy.

"Look at the car. Do you see anything wrong with it?"

I walked around it. "No, looks great."

"Feel the inside wall of the left front tire."

I reached around and found a humongous bulge.

"Guy who owned it bounced it off a curb. We turned the tire inside out."

"Isn't that kind'a dangerous?"

"Yeah. If a mark sees it. It might clue 'em in about the front end."

"The front end?"

"It's shot."

"Really? You going to sell it like that?"

"Sure!" Cost me a G-note to fix it.

"Don't you think someone will notice on a test drive?"

"Sure they'll notice something. You tell 'em it needs an alignment. Say we'll put it in the shop, tighten it up so it runs better - for a while. By then it's theirs."

"Is that shmoozing?"

"Yeah, but I got a better example."

His eyes took on a glint as he rubbed his hands together.

"This'll get you an extra five-hundred bucks, easy. When the mark makes an offer, tell 'em there's already a deal subject to financing that expires at four p.m. tomorrow. The next day call him and say the guy didn't show. But he's coming in today after five with the dough. But now, since the deal expired, it's a first come first serve situation. If he matches the other guy's offer it's his."

"You do that?"

"Works great! And the guy's so rushed, he overlooks all the little defects until the papers are signed and we're off the hook."

"That's shmoozing?"

"At its finest."

"Very interesting."

"Well, kid, When can you start?"

"Oh, I wasn't here about a job. I was thinking about buying this car. But I'm no longer interested."

He stood there for a moment. I could almost hear the gears changing in his head. Then he took my arm.

"Well, I've got a nice little Z\28 Camaro, owned by a kindygarten teacher up in Anchorage. Never been winter driven!"

Nice recovery Vinnie, but in this case, you shmooze -- you lose.

Ergo, The Egomobile

You know, sometimes I wish I was a mechanic instead of a writer. Especially when I get the bill. The Honda I own now is not a problem. It was the contraption I owned before the Honda that was the problem. It has a marquee that'll put dollar signs in any mechanics eyes -- Porsche.

I bought it for therapeutic reasons -- to massage my ego.

I only paid six grand for it. It's wasn't expensive as far as Porsches go. Until it died on me that is. Well, it didn't really die. It was more like a coma. A death I could handle. But the life support this thing needed nearly killed something else of mine. My checking account.

To my dismay, I could only find one shop within forty miles that would even touch the thing.

"Sure," he said on the phone. "Bring it on in. I'll take care of you."

He took care of me all right.

TUESDAY JANUARY 9.

"Battery wasn't taking a charge."

"It wasn't?" I asked.

"Nope. So, I replaced it."

"Oh, okay. So when will it be ready?" I asked.

"Something's still not right. I wanna check it out. Call me tomorrow."

WEDNESDAY JANUARY 10.

"You're ballast resistor's shot, gotta replace it."

"Will it be ready today?" I asked.

"Parts coming from Buffalo. It'll be here Tuesday."

"Tuesday! As in next week?"

"They'll ship it tomorrow. It'll be three days in transit, then the weekend. If we're lucky should have it Tuesday afternoon. Call me next Wednesday."

WEDNESDAY JANUARY 17.

"It's still not quite right," he said.

"Can you narrow that down a bit?"

"Battery's still not charging. Might be your alternator."

"Great." Three days from Buffalo for a lousy resistor, where are they going to have to send for an alternator -- Hamburg?

"Believe it or not, they got one in town."

"REALLY?!" What a surprise.

"But it's not cheap."

Like I said, what a surprise. "What's, not cheap?"

"It's kind of an odd ball. Could run about three hundred."

"DOLLARS?!"

"But, I tell you what. I'll send yours out to a jobber and get it rebuilt. Maybe I can save you some dough."

"How long will that take?"

"Who knows? Call me Monday."

MONDAY JANUARY 22.

"Can't rebuild the alternator. I'll have to put in a new one."

"Great. Okay, so what do you think, tomorrow afternoon?"

"Nope. They sold the one in town. I'm gonna have to freight one in from Hamburg."

"How long will that take?"

"Depends if you want me to ship it regular freight or

express?"

"What's regular?"

"A Liberian cargo carrier that docks in New York a week Thursday. Then they ship it to Chicago by train. And then out here on the bus and a courier delivers it to my shop."

"What's express?"

"I pick it up at the bus station."

"Is that extra?"

"Only 20 bucks."

"What the hell. Let's shoot the works."

"Call me a week Thursday."

THURSDAY FEBRUARY 6.

"Yeah, got the alternator in, but there's a problem with your timing."

I'll say.

"I think it's your distributor."

"Speaking of distributors, where is this coming form?"

"Mexico. It'll be through customs Tuesday. Come on in on Thursday. It might be ready."

THURSDAY, FEBRUARY 13, D-DAY (DEBT-DAY).

". . . and with the lubrication system analysis . . . ."

"What does that mean?"

"We checked your oil."

"Oh."

"With tax, that comes to $1678.63."

"What!?"

"Hey, you're lucky I didn't charge you storage."

Driven To Lust

Some men fool around on their wives. I buy cars instead. You could say I'm automotively promiscuous. I'll drive anything with wheels.

I've had 32 cars in my life. I think you'll agree, that's quite a few.

I stayed with one for five years. One lasted only overnight. I've even had three going at the same time.

Sometimes I'll go to a car lot just so I can test drive something new, get a little variety. I've even driven friends' cars on the pretense mine was in the shop. I'm just terrible.

They say you never forget your first car. Mine was a '66 Chrysler Windsor. They don't make car's like that anymore. Heck, they don't make aircraft carriers like that anymore.

She got about eight gallons to the mile and we drove nearly every chance we got. She was big, comfortable and easy to drive. The perfect car to break in an innocent 16-year-old. Eventually, I found a little '67 Chevy II I liked better.

My favorite was my '68 Formula 'S' Barracuda. The 'Cuda had 325 horsepower and a 150 mile per hour speedometer teasing me to test her limits. Her raw power was seductive and driving her was intoxicating. Speed was our drug. One day we overdosed and fried her heads.

But the biggest mistake I ever made was getting involved with that darn Porsche.

But still, even after all the problems I'd had, it was hard to let her go once the spark had gone. I mean, how do you break up with a car?

"Porsche."

"Yes, Brock?"

"We have to talk."

"Can't we just *drive,* instead?" she purred.

"No. We can't." I replied, firm in my resolve.

"Has my insurance expired?"

"No."

"Well, get in. Let's drive."

I reached for the handle, then pulled away. "No."

"Come on. Grip my wheel, thrust my shifter into gear, make me accelerate."

"Cut it out! Drive, drive, drive! Doesn't anyone ever park anymore? Look, it's been great," I lied, "but I just I can't afford you anymore."

"Afford me!? You haven't spent a dime on me all week."

"Oh Yeah! Just yesterday you were squealing at me to replace your brakes."

"Well, new shoes would be nice for a change."

"And in the morning you're so bloody cranky."

"That's just typical. You jump in and expect me to turn over and perform without warming me up. Then when I cough a couple of times, you're the one who gets choked."

"Look, we just can't go on like this," I said.

"Name one good reason."

"One more repair and I'm going to have to take out a second mortgage."

"Okay, name one more reason."

"Well," I said, "the neighbors are starting to talk for one thing."

"About you and I?"

"Only the fact that I'm standing in my driveway having a conversation with my car."

"Talk's not what I'm interested in."

"You're right. Talk's cheap. Cheap is one thing you are definitely not."

Well, that was it. The darn thing blew a gasket on me and seized right on the spot. I was now the owner neighborhood's most expensive lawn ornament.

When the tow truck pulled away my, wife put a sympathetic arm around me.

"You know," I said to her, "I feel like a piece of me is gone with her."

"I feel the same way," my wife replied.

"You do?"

"Sure. After all, we have a joint checking account."

The Squeaky Wheel

After eight years my wife's old Pontiac finally passed on to the great parking lot in the sky. The kids cried, my wife sobbed, and I said a few unprintable words as the wrecker towed it to its final reward. As far as I was concerned, it got what it deserved!

So there we were, marooned in suburbia without a family car. I knew it was only a matter of time before my wife went absolutely berserk and ended up in a tower with a high-caliber rifle.

"SUBURBAN HOMEMAKER KILLS 86, FILM AT ELEVEN."

No, something had to be done and done quickly. We knew we wanted a mini-van, but I didn't have time to shop around. So it was up to Terri alone. Within a couple of days she called me at work.

"I found one. And it's only eleven nine!"

I booked off work and met her at the dealership for a test drive. It was great! It had a V-6 to pull our trailer, air conditioning for those hot summer days, and tinted glass so I could swat the kids without being spotted.

We spent an hour going over it and decided this was the one for us.

"Okay," my wife said to the salesman, "we'll take it."

He wrote up the deal, took it to the sales manager and returned with a worried look.

"No go," he said. "He wants fifteen."

It was at that point Terri blew a gasket. "What!? You told me on the phone the price was eleven nine," she said, incredulous.

"That was the price last week. The sale is over."

"Right!" She shoved him out of the way, stomped over to the sales manager's office, snatched the phone from his hand, and slammed the receiver into its cradle.

She now had his full attention.

"Your salesman told me the advertised price was eleven nine. I offered eleven nine cash and now you have the unmitigated gall to try and gouge another three grand out of me. To top it off, this wasted my time, and cost me and my husband money because we both had to leave work. Not to mention all the other things I've put off to come down here on good faith!"

A small crowd of sales people and customers gathered in the showroom, peering in the direction of Terri's tirade.

She put her hands on the sales manager's desk and leaned in inches from his face. "So here's what I'm going to do. I going to call the Department of Consumer Affairs and inform them of your trade practices. Then I'm going to call the Motor Dealer Licensing Branch and inform them you have no sticker prices on your cars; a clear violation. Then I'm going to write letters to the editor about this to every paper within a hundred miles. And finally my husband is going to include this incident in his syndicated column and send a copy to your corporate office so they can see what a great job you're doing." She left him sitting there, his lower jaw hanging somewhere around his ankles.

A short while later, Terri called me at work.

"Guess what. When I got home there was a message

on the machine. It was that sales manager. He said we can have the van for eleven nine."

"Did he say anything else?" I asked, expecting a full apology.

"Yes. He wants to know where we'd like it delivered."

Okay, That'll do.

Do Bank Machines Dream Electric Sheep?

When bank machines first appeared I thought they were a good idea. Now, I'm not so sure.

I've had a few problems with them. Like the time I made a payment on my credit line and darn near paid off the national debt.

Or when I tried to muddle through after mistakenly selecting French instead of English at an airport location. By the time I finished, it took three accountants and a senior programmer from IBM six weeks to discover I'd converted my life savings into Drachmas and transferred them to a daily interest account at the First Peoples Bank of Gdansk.

My wife was ticked about that one. You should have heard her. "Do you know what a lousy interest rate you get in daily savings accounts?"

Then, there was last week when I went to make a withdrawal. I inserted my card and waited for the screen to start the familiar series of messages. But to my surprise, there was a voice instead.

"Select language please."

"Uh, English," I said, not wanting a repeat trip to Poland.

"Good-day, Brockton J. Macdonald."

Yeah, like I'm supposed to respond, "Hello, bank machine. How's the CPU and chips?"

"Enter your security code now."

I did. I can't tell what it is. I trust you, but it's something unprintable. I figured that way, I wouldn't forget it.

"You know," said the machine, "that's disgusting."

"Yeah, well it works for me," I replied.

"Fine," it shot back. "What would you like to do?"

"Withdrawal."

"Withdrawal from what?"

"Huh?"

"From which type of account?" it asked, clearly losing patience.

"Savings."

"Savings, huh? What type of savings?"

"I don't know, the kind you put money in."

"Listen, Bud . . . ."

"That's Brock!"

"Whatever. We've got sixteen different types of savings accounts."

"Okay, so look up my record."

"What do I look like, a file clerk?"

"For crying out loud! Forget it, just give me my card back."

"Why should I?"

"Huh?"

"How do I know you really are Brockton J. Macdonald?"

"Hey, I punched in my code, remember?"

"Hey, you could've punched him until he gave it to you."

"This is ridiculous."

"Got any ID?"

"What?"

"Hold your drivers license up to my camera."

"Forget it. Just give me my card back."

"No ID, no card."

"This isn't happening," I said, as I pulled out my wallet and held my license to the camera. "There, satisfied?"

"Ugh. You're not really photogenic, are you?"

"Just give me the card you 8-bit half-wit!"

"Okay, okay." It spit out the card in two pieces. "OOPS! Did I do that?"

I stood there, yelling my code at it, for a half hour before I stormed off.

Now I finally understand the meaning of artificial intelligence

Express Yourself

I'm one of those people who follow the rules. I never pass on a double solid line, I never run the goalie in the end boards, and I never try to take more than nine items through the express line at the grocery store.

So when I'm standing in line, with my nine or less, and someone's in front of me with ten or more, I get a little choked.

I'd love to see, just once, the cashier get on the PA and call, "Security to the express line, security to the express line please . . . ."

The other day I was waiting in the express line and the guy in front of me had more than nine items in his basket. Now, I was in a hurry. I'm not usually in a hurry because, hey, I like to take life casually. But, that day, I was in a hurry.

So I got to thinking. Here I am standing in the express line, in a hurry, and this dope in front of me has more than nine items in his basket. I could have broken the speed limit to get here, but Noooo. I could have parked in the handicap spot right by the door, but Noooo.

I started to think about all the other things that tick me off. Guys who let their dogs fertilize my lawn. Children who scream for no reason. Idiots who let their kids play with fireworks. Litter bugs, tailgaters, book burners, thieves, liars, wife beaters!

All the years of putting up with rule breakers finally

got to me and I wasn't going to take it anymore. When this guy unloaded his basket I was going to say, "HEY!" and point up to the sign above the register. "This is the express line! It says NINE ITEMS OR LESS, NO CHECKS! What's the matter with you, pal? CAN'T YOU READ?!"

I watched and counted and when he put the tenth item on the counter I was ready. But the cashier beat me to it.

"Excuse me, sir," she said. "This is express only, nine items or less."

Yes! YES! Finally someone caught, YES!

"Oh," he replied. "I'm sorry," and he put the TV Guide back in the rack. "There, that's nine." She rang him through.

That's it? I felt let down.

I plunked my order on the counter. Darn, so close.

"That's $21.63 please," she said.

I opened my wallet and found only a ten and two fives. Oh, oh!

"I seem to be a little short, uh, could I, uh, maybe write a check?"

"Security to the express line! Security to the express line please . . . ."

"Look Martha!" came a voice from the line behind me, "they caught someone!"

"Yahoo!" whooped Martha. "Fry the sucker!"

A Novel Idea

Working at home is an ideal situation. Then again . . . .

Having some time on my hands, I decided to concentrate on writing that novel I always knew I had in me.

I entered my home office, shut the door, faced the monitor, and became one with the keyboard.

It was . . . .

KNOCK! KNOCK! KNOCK! "Dad! Have you seen my shoes?!"

"Go away. I'm working."

"Oh, sorry. MOM. . . !"

I turned back to the screen.

It was a . . . .

RING!

"Can someone get that?"

RING!

"Get the phone please?!"

RING!

"Would someone PLEASE . . .?!"

RING!

"For crying out loud! HELLO!"

"Good morning! I'm selling subscriptions to . . . ."

"I can't read." CLICK! "Okay, Where was I?"

It was a dark . . . .

DING DONG!

"Can someone get the door?"

DING DONG!

"There's someone at the door!"

DING DONG!

"Would someone PLEASE . . .?!"

DING DONG!

"For crying out loud!"

"Good-day," said one of the magazine-toting women. "Do you think there will be peace in your life-time?"

"Not if this morning is any indication."

"We'd like to discuss . . . ."

"Wait a sec! Do you represent some sort of religious group?"

"Why, yes."

"That's taken care of. I'm a practicing Druid. Care to stay for the human sacrifice we're having later?"

They quickly clicked away in their sensible shoes.

"Okay, let's try this again."

It was a dark and stormy . . . .

My office door flew open. "Honey, look after the boy while I vacuum." In came the seven-year-old who went directly to my computer and pushed reset.

"NO! WAIT! You little &*$%#!

DING DONG!

"Somebody get the door!"

DING DONG!

"Somebody please get the. . . !"

DING DONG!

I flung open the door. "WHAT?!"

"We had a complaint about human sacrifice," said the police officer. "Know anything about that?"

"Maybe."

"I'll have to take you in."

"I'll get my notebook."

Finally, a quiet place to write. By the time they found

my lawyer and he sobered up enough to get me out, I figured I could get at least the first chapter written.

It was a dark and stormy night!

Murder He Wrote

My friend, Arthur, murders people.

Well, he doesn't really murder them. He writes about murdering them. Arthur's a mystery writer. You might say Arthur authors them to death.

No, of course you wouldn't.

Anyway, Arthur has a unique way of doing research. He brings people with different backgrounds into his study to make malevolent and murderous speculations in an anything goes brainstorming session. Then he uses the ideas bandied about for his stories.

Arthur made introductions, then asked, "Haven't you wanted to kill somebody at sometime?"

We all nodded because, after all, who hasn't wanted to throttle someone at one time or another?

"What we have here," he said, "is a very creative serial killer who murders people representative of those we love to hate."

"You mean like politicians?" asked Brenda, the librarian.

"Or used car salesmen?" asked Carl, the carpenter.

"Exactly," confirmed Arthur. "What you have to do is pick the victims and the method of their demise."

"I have a thought," I said. "Wouldn't it be ironic if the manner of death fit the occupation of the victim?"

They all seemed to like that idea and soon the ideas were flowing.

"How about the cook at a staff cafeteria," offered Val, the secretary. "He eats his own slop and dies of food poisoning."

"A postal clerk!" said Moira, the RN "A postal clerk gets a paper cut and bleeds to death waiting in line at the emergency ward."

"Or make it a Department of Motor Vehicle clerk," said Vince, the cabby.

"Interchangeable," we all agreed.

"AM radio deejays!" said Brenda. "Tie one in a chair and force her to listen to rap music until her brain explodes."

"The Senate!" said Carl. "The whole works of them could get bit by tsetse flies and die of sleeping sickness."

"Weather forecasters!" said Vince. "One goes out fishing after hearing a report of favorable conditions only to be drowned in a typhoon."

"Speaking of typhoons how about a mime!" said Brenda.

"Definitely!" said Carl, as everyone enthusiastically nodded in agreement.

"A mime swept away by gale force winds with an audience watching and applauding from inside at such a realistic performance."

I was just about to make my first suggestion when someone blurted out -- "A humorist!"

"YES! I hate those condescending, snickering snots!" cried someone else. "Tape a respirator to his face, feed him nitrous oxide, then read him his own writing until he laughs himself to death."

They all looked at me. I could see the menace in their eyes.

"Now calm down everyone," said Arthur. "This is all for fun. Besides, it wouldn't work. I've read his work and

it's not that funny."
    "How about critics," I said . . . .

Pseudo Modern Neo-Experimentalism

I may not know art, but I know a good joke when I hear one. When I heard that Canada's National Gallery acquired Voice Of Fire, a painting consisting of three vertical stripes of paint in two different colors, for $10 million, I was reminded of a story about some prominent art critics. They were presented with an abstract and after praising it as a work of genius, were told it had been done by a chimpanzee. Hey, $10 million will buy a lot of bananas.

So this philistine decided he should know more about abstract expressionism. It's one thing to criticize. But to ridicule you, really have to know what you're talking about.

I went down to a local art school and invited three artists out for lunch if they'd further my education in modern art. They readily accepted. Starving artists never turn down free food. Free anything for that matter.

Kaitlin specialized in seascapes, Kim worked in water colors, and Fred was an abstract expressionist.

"So," I said, "tell me about abstract expressionism."

I expected an informative discussion amongst the group, but what I got was a thirty minute dissertation from Fred.

"... See? There really is no question," he said. "Abstract

art is art for the sake of art. When you buy an abstract, you're not buying canvas and paint."

"You're not?" I asked.

"No, you're buying a piece of the artist's soul bared on the canvas for all to see."

The others rolled their eyes and reached for their drinks.

"Tell you what." I said. "Lets try a little experiment. Each of you give me a painting, I'll anonymously arrange for them to be displayed at a consignment gallery with instructions to get whatever they can for them. Then after a couple of days, I'll try to buy them."

Before the other two could react Fred slapped his hand on the table. "Agreed! This will prove there is no comparison to abstract art."

That, I knew already.

A few days later I walked into the gallery and started negotiations with the dealer.

The first painting was a seascape by Kaitlin.

"How much do you want for this?" I asked.

"That particular work is $450," she replied.

"Wow, that's a lot. I quite like it though. Say, how much is that one worth?" I asked, pointing at Kim's water color of a Chinese dragon.

"It's worth is relative, wouldn't you say? The price, however, is $650."

"Gosh, wild colors?"

"Quite."

"Hmmmm. How about that thing over there?" I asked pointing to the work by Fred, the abstract expressionist.

"Let me propose this," she said. "If you purchase the other two, I'll throw this one in."

"What! You'd give away a part of someone's soul?" I

asked.

"The only sole connected here is when the artist painted the bottom of his shoes and trampled on the canvas."

"Sold!" I said.

What the heck. I love Kim and Kaitlin's stuff. And Fred's thing, it makes for a great door mat.

To Sleep, Per Chance
To Scream

Back when I was a technical writer, I went to a customer service seminar as a last minute substitution for someone who was smart enough to call in sick.

Tech writers, like myself, never even see a customer, let alone service one. But, there I was, in a room full of bright, bubbly, enthusiastically extroverted, customer-service types.

On any other day this wouldn't be a problem, but not that day. You see, I'd played hockey until two in the morning, blew a fourteen-game scoring streak, and the Barbarian brothers, who were out on parole, mugged me in a corner after an icing call. I felt wretched.

I was tired, I was depressed, and I was sure I was nursing a few cracked ribs. The last place I wanted to be was around a bunch of bright, bubbly, enthusiastically extroverted, customer-service types insisting everyone have a nice day.

I wasn't going to have a nice day. I was going to have a rotten day, no matter how strongly they persisted. I didn't want to have a day at all. I wanted to sleep through the whole thing.

The table at the back was empty. I sank into a chair and laid my head on my arms and soon felt myself slipping into blissful slumber.

The sudden tapping on my arm sat me bolt upright, sending sharp pains through my side.

"Hello!" said a bright, bubbly, enthusiastically extroverted, customer-service-type woman sitting beside me.

"What? What is it?" I asked, grimacing in pain. "Is the building on fire?"

"No, silly! The seminar is starting! Time to get up sleepy head!" she chimed musically, pinching my cheek.

"If I ignore you will you go away?" I asked, putting my down again.

"It's no wonder you're here if you're always this rude to people who talk to you?" she said with a smile.

"Only when they talk in my sleep," I replied.

I heard the lecturer on stage clear his throat and ask, "Anyone find these seminars boring? Come on, raise your hand."

My bright, bubbly, enthusiastically extroverted customer-service-type neighbor must have interpreted my sleeping for boredom. And not wanting me to miss the chance to participate, she tried to gain my attention by taking her elbow and jabbing it into my ribs.

I remember hearing a crack just before the blinding flash of pain, then only fleeting images until I found myself horizontal in hospital.

The pain was excruciating, I could hardly breath, but at least I was in a bed.

I closed my eyes and gingerly rolled over on my good side.

Then I heard squeaky shoes coming down the corridor. They got louder and louder until they squeaked right up to my bed.

"All right!" said the bright, bubbly, enthusiastically extroverted, health-care type. "Wake up call! Time for your sleeping pill."

I was incredulous.

"You sure you don't want to give me an enema too?"

"Not now, sweetie. I'll get you up in a couple of hours for that."

In A Word

Sometimes I wonder why people make such a fuss about language. Language is for communication. As long as you can do that, what's the big deal if you're speaking English, Spanish or Swahili? There are times at my house I'm not sure what language we're speaking. But somehow we always manage to get the message across.

For instance, the first thing I say when the smoke detector goes of is, "toast's up", because that's what it usually means. So we refer to out First Alert as the toast alert.

What really sets the darn thing off is the *bark*. That's the end of the loaf.

Although it has been known to go off when someone's *frazzling* (frying) and few *rounds* (links) of *oinks* (sausages).

Now if you look outside and the sky is dark and gray then it's a *blurmy* day. If it's raining too, then it's a *glurmy* day.

If you're going out to a restaurant or a party and the occasion doesn't quite warrant a tie, but jeans are out, then you dress *drasualy*.

And in such a situation you might be running a little late, like my wife usually is after she's *flitted* (tried on) the fourteenth outfit and still doesn't know what to wear. Then she becomes extremely *flustrated*.

But being *flustrated* is not uncommon in a house with small children because, after all, it is a rather *hect-*

ive life style. Like when we have guests and the *boy* (preschooler) is running around as a *noonie* (naked). This is not to be confused with a *nooner,* which how we got the kid in the first place.

Children do grow up though, eventually mutating into fashion conscious teenagers, and become *nephrotytes,* which is a person who looks pretty good, but doesn't do a heck of a lot.

That is unless they're not good looking and a little short of gray matter, then they qualify as a *hidiot.*

Speaking of low intelligence, if you're a typical urban driver, zipping in and out of traffic at twice the posted speed limit in your *ozone eater* (car), you are what I refer to as an *insaniac.*

Then, when I arrive home after an hour on the *parkade* (the highway at rush hour), all I get for dinner is *mustgoes.* Those are all the leftovers in the fridge that simply must go.

If we're going to the *co-parent's* (your kid's best friends parents) house for dinner, then I can be sure of being served scrud, which is just about anything they cook.

How about the week before school when I took my daughter to meet her grade one teacher. They *quibbed* (verbal exchange of information) for a few minutes and then the teacher said, "So, Krissy, what does your dad do?"

"My dad? Oh, he's just a *wordo.*"

Arrested Thoughts

Just when you think it can't possibly get any sillier than it already is, the forces of inane stupidity strike again.

Yes, it's the continuing adventures of the dreaded, politically correct, word police.

Here's what happened.

I was listening to a radio talk show and the host was interviewing a woman representing a bicycle advocacy group.

Mr. Talk-show-host asked if she was in favor of a safety program being, "mandatory".

To which she replied, that that word [mandatory] was no longer used. It had been replaced with the term, "universally available".

HELLO! EXCUSE ME?

Now I'm sure it's as obvious to you as it is to me, [and it certainly was to Mr. Talk-show-host] "universally available" is nowhere close to meaning the same thing as "mandatory".

If something is "mandatory", you've got no choice in the matter. It's a done deal.

However, if something is "universally available" then it's more of an option whether you choose to use it or not.

I.e.: brains are mandatory; using them is universally available.

See what I mean?

Now if that representative had used her, "universally available" option, she might have realized that by pushing the politically correct envelope to the point of the ridiculous, she had totally taken away from her group's message.

I can't even remember what the message was now. All I remember is "mandatory" was deemed not politically correct and precise and clear language took another beating in the PC attack on freedom of speech.

Could have used "compulsory."

Could have used "required."

Nope. "Universally available."

It's bad enough they try to tell us how and what parts of the English language we can use. The least they could do is to come up with an alternative that has the same meaning.

Being a writer I get a little defensive about the tools of my trade; especially when non-writers start fiddling about with something as fundamental as definitions. Webster must be turning in the grave.

I don't have a problem with gender neutral terms. I prefer chair instead of chairman, and firefighter rather than fireman.

But what sense does it make to not use words that begin with "man"? Think about it.

One day the word police could manage a mandate to maneuver a maniacal manuscripted manifesto of manipulation to manufacture a manifold of manners to mantle, mangle, and manacle our very thoughts.

But then, I couldn't say that, could I?

Slango Tango

Now that we're nearing the 21st century, let's see how you've kept up with pop-culture slang. You know what they say, "if you're not hip, you're a drip." Which is the correct meaning?

1. Boomer:

a. Teenager with a ghettoblaster.

b. Person born during the post-war baby boom.

c. A ballistic missile nuclear submarine.

2. Pinheads:

a. Members of the Senate.

b. Groupies of the pro-bowler's tour.

c. People who collect souvenir pins.

3. Ecotage:

a. French council for economic diversification.

b. Multi-source reverberations in rap music.

c. Pro-environmental terrorist acts.

4. Fuzz word:

a. Buzz words that fade quickly from use.

b. The way pro athletes talk *"you know"*.

c. A precise sounding word that's meaning remains fuzzy. Used mostly in Washington.

5. Vanilla:

a. A huge Spanish garage for recreational vehicles.

b. A disease inflicting game-show letter-turners.

c. Absolutely and utterly basic.

6. House:

a. Something most people can't afford.

b. Head, as in, your brain *house*.

c. Great performance. As in, he *housed* the place.

7. Key:

a. Something to start with, until you can afford the house.

b. Descramblers for adult channels on satellite

c. The best, as in, Cam Neely is a *Key* Bruin.

8. PT Boat:

a. What you need one of to sink the Canadian Navy.

b. The thing the Canadian Navy fears the most.

c. A quick defenceman with offensive skills.

9. Wetware:

a. The new anti-aids device - body condoms.

b. Clothing worn in the Northwest between September and June.

c. Computer-geek jargon for your brain.

10. Wunk:

a. Sound of Ross Perot hitting the bottom of the polls.

b. A goaltender's favorite sound (puck into glove).

c. Sixties teen music, or wasp funk.

11. Gorilla:

a. An IRS auditor.

b. Construction workers who spends more time whistling at women than working.

c. A blockbuster film.

12. Glock:

a. A 48-hour clock.

b. A dip in stock prices, as in - glitch.

c. Metal-detector proof ceramic pistol.

Easy scoring on this. In each case the correct answer was, c. For those of you who didn't get at least 10 you've got until the rest of the decade to get up to speed. But, of course, by then, you'll have to start all over again.

The Chicken Or The Egg

For everything we have now there was a first. So as a little reminder, here are a few famous first, and the not so famous firsts that followed.

First: The first regularly scheduled airline flight was January 1, 1914, from Tampa Bay to St. Petersburg, Florida.

First that followed: Jan. 2, 1914 -- lost luggage claim by Arvil D. Struppmyer. The bags were eventually located in Buffalo Springs, Montana, Jan. 3, 1978.

First: The first bank, opened by goldsmith, Lawrence Hoare, began accepting deposits in London, June 7, 1633.

First that followed: June 8, 1633 -- The first service charge for withdrawal from a saving account paid by Quigly J. Leek.

First: The first candy bar was sold March 17, 1853, in Bristol, England as Fry's Cream Stick.

First that followed: March 18, 1853 -- Dr. Arthur P. Schmendrickton of Bristol, recorded the first case of acne.

First: The first car manufacturer, Karl Benz of Mannheim, Germany, sold his first unit September 8, 1888.

First that followed: September 9, 1888 - 60 miles outside Mannheim, Germany, Derwin G. Plutz made the first call to the first auto club to inquire when someone would open the first gas station.

First: The first practical programmable computer was exhibited by George Shultz of Stockholm, Sweden at the

Paris World's Fair, July 2, 1855.

First that followed: July 2, 1855 -- David Doyle Glitch, attending the Paris World's fair became the first computer nerd.

First: The first divorce was between Edward and Margaret Barr on May 8, 1546.

First that followed: May 8, 1546, the first divorce settlement, followed closely by the first petition for personal bankruptcy.

First: The first electric light for domestic use was by Moses G. Farmer who lit his home in Salem, Massachusetts, November 1879, with a platinum burner lamp.

First that followed: Dec. 1879, the first utility bill for $206.67 issued to Massachusetts resident M.G. Farmer.

First: The first Post Office opened in England on Nov. 17, 1619.

First that followed: Nov. 18, 1619, first use of the phrase, "The check is in the mail."

First: The first organized hockey game was played at Victoria Park Skating Rink in Montreal on March 3, 1875, between F.W. Terrence's team and J.G.A. Creighton's team.

First that followed: Mar. 3, 1875, first reported incident of a donnybrook. Witnesses were reported to say the event was spectacular but asked, "What's that little black thing for?"

It

Every generation has a fashion statement that in retrospect is a total embarrassment.

It is always the same. No one knows how *It* starts. But, once *It* does it's to late to do anything about *It*. Even tracing *Its* origins to point a finger of blame is a gesture in futility. Once started there's no stopping *It* as those involved behave like lemmings jumping off the cliff of peer pressure to die on the jagged rocks of fashion humiliation below.

History is replete with transgressions of the past. *It* was zoot suits in the forties, *It* was raccoon skin hats in the fifties, *It* was bell bottoms in the sixties, and *It* was platform shoes in the seventies.

But that's nothing compared to what *It* is now.

It is dominant in every mall and every high school in the land. *It* is anywhere young people congregate. *It* is everywhere.

It has been called, the geek look, the I-don't-know-if-I'm-coming-or-going look, and the brain-damaged-Arkansas-backcatcher look.

This time *It* is wearing one's baseball hat backwards.

In my day, anyone who insisted on wearing his hat like that would have been labeled as slow and sent to a special school.

What does this, as a fashions statement, say, 'Look at me, I'm a total idiot' maybe?

What else would anyone be who spends thirty dollars on an article of clothing and wears it backwards?

Why buy an outrageously overpriced baseball hat, filling the pockets of greedy, pro-sports, franchise owners, only to wear it in a way no one can see it unless you're their chauffeur?

Maybe *It* fills the adolescent need to rebel against authority, against the status quo, against the norm; the need to strive toward independence by acting like a total moron.

There is no practical reason to wear a hat in this manner, unless you live with a morbid fear of rain trickling down your neck. So why do it?

Think about this for a minute. What's to follow? Wearing other articles of clothing backwards? Will we see young men wondering aimlessly in malls with their coats on backwards, cultivating the straight-jacket look?

If they did, there'd be no reason to wear a crested T-shirt, unless it was on backwards too.

Apply this devolution in fashion mutation to footwear and the implications are too bizarre to even contemplate.

Will young women, in an attempt at fashion equity, start wearing pony tails at the front? Or totally confuse the entire male adolescent population by wearing their bras in reverse.

This fad, as others before, will eventually die a deserving death and fade into the shadows of memory.

But in twenty years, when old scrap books are hauled out of the closet, or an archaic home video is fed into a machine, the questions will be asked, "Dad, did you used to be retarded?"

Phraseology

When I was a corporate business writer I worked with a guy called, Myron.

You'd walk by and ask, "How are you doing, Myron?" and get an answer like, "Performance is peak!" or "Got an even keel."

I couldn't figure what the deal was with him until Ted, another manager, approached me with a Newsletter he'd found on Myron's desk called, *Power Phrasing*, from the National Association For Effective Middle Management.

"Can you reproduce this on your computer and substitute the 'Phrases of the month' with these?" He handed me a sheet.

"Yeah, sure. What's going on?"

"You'll see."

Next day, I waited in the boardroom with the project team. An unusual amount of smirks were luring about. Seemed everyone was in on Ted's little joke.

Finally, Myron walked in, but so did the CEO.

The smirks quickly went away.

Ted turned pale and stuck his pipe in his mouth.

"Gentleman," said the CEO, "we've got a problem. The client thinks he wants a competitor's system. We must convince him otherwise."

"You can lead a horse to water," said Myron, "but you can't make him do the back stroke."

The CEO raised a brow. "Well said young man. What's

your name?"

"Myron, sir."

Ted bit down on the stem of his pipe with a crunch.

"We'll feed him so much information," the CEO continued. "He'll have to rely on our recommendations."

"If you can't convince them," said Myron, "confuse them."

"Exactly!" said the CEO.

Ted stroked his beard nervously.

"He must think only we can help him."

"An ounce of image is worth a pound of performance," said Myron.

"Very perceptive, Myron," said the CEO.

Ted buried his face in his hands.

"We have to come up with something now!"

"Any plan today is better than a perfect plan tomorrow," offered Myron.

"Right!" said the CEO. "Now we need someone to take the ball and run with it."

"If you want a track team to win," said Myron, "you find a guy who can jump eight feet, not eight guys who can jump a foot."

"Capital, Myron! Capital! Come with me."

The next week, Ted came by my desk. "Did you hear? They made Myron vice-president of projects. He's running the whole darn show now!"

"I wouldn't worry," I said. "I don't think he'll last too long."

"Why's that?"

"Did see the memo he posted?"

"No, what's it say."

"It says, 'The greatest myth about sound management is that it actually exists'."

Cross Dressers

I don't usually go to press conferences, unless there's a no-host bar. But this one caught my attention. The National Association for Effective Middle Management had something to say about sexism in the work place.

Now as everyone knows, the organization with the acronym that sounds like someone clearing their throat, NAEMM, is the farm team for the old-boys network. So, when they address a subject like sexism, I'm all ears. Even without the free scotch.

I gathered with the rest of the media when NAEMM's chair, Arthur P. Schmendrickton, took the podium.

"We at NAEMM feel there is a great injustice in the work place. By gross inaction, an unwritten code has evolved seriously repressing an entire gender, forcing managers to adhere to a practice based on their sex. But that will all change. For today we announce our campaign: DEFEM."

"What does that stand for?" asked someone up front.

"Dress Equality For Every Manager!" He turned to the screen where a picture flashed up of a young woman.

"Notice how her hair is coifed to perfection." A series of pictures clicked on. "See? A new hair style for every day of the week if desired." Then a collage of five different men -- all with the same hair cut. "But us? No! We are expected to conform and comply to this unwritten and sexist code or else!" The picture on the screen changed to a man in a green mohawk standing in an unemployment line.

"But the real injustice is this," he said, as another picture flashed up of a middle-aged woman, dressed in a loose blouse, long, flowing skirt, and flat, open-toed sandals. "While women are allowed, by this unspoken code, to wear comfortable clothes in the work place, men are stuck with this," he stated, as a picture lit up of a middle-aged man beading with perspiration in a dark-gray suit, button-down shirt, a tie, and black brogues. "Have you ever tried to sit through a three-hour meeting in a rig like that and still keep your wits? It's impossible! No wonder women are making us look so bad in the boardrooms of the nation."

"Are you suggesting men should wear skirts to work?" asked someone, with a chuckle.

"No! Not at all," he replied.

"Then what's your point?"

"That this is discrimination. And the only way there will be true equality in the work place is for women to conform to the dress code forced upon men."

"In other words . . . ?"

"In other words we want women to wear the same tortuous wool suits, tight suffocating collars and ties that men do."

I don't know. I kind of liked the skirt idea. At least in my case, I could get away with a kilt.

Unemployment Enjoyment

There are lots of handbooks available on how to get a job. But you won't find any information on how not to get a job.

I mean, after all, who wants to give up those great unemployment benefits. It's not just the money. It's the lifestyle, right?

Think of all the free time.

You can stay up and watch the late, late, late show. Maybe roll out of bed for a leisurely brunch, then wander down to the rink for a skate with the UI hockey team. Or head to the local links for a few rounds in the UI Open.

No, the last thing you need is a job, especially in the summer. Think of that great tan you can work on while your foolish friends slave away in some office, or die of heat exhaustion flipping burgers over a hot grill.

Now understand that you have to look for work and send resumes out. That's expected. But don't worry, no decent employer is going to hire you just for sending out a resume. You can still ensure your unemployment enjoyment during that big obstacle in the job search -- the interview.

FIVE IMPORTANT INTERVIEW TIPS

1. Show up late:

This might keep you safely unemployed by itself.

Being late leaves a very bad impression on a prospective employer and is a good opening gambit. Always have a good excuse ready such as, "Sorry I'm late, but my license is suspended for DUI, so I had to hitch hike".

2. Dress and act inappropriately:

If the situation requires a suit, wear jeans. Smoke if you're so inclined or chew gum. Don't forget to point out your really cool body pierces. Bring a Walkman and wear the headphones at all times. Not only will this almost guarantee you won't get hired, it could save you valuable leisure time in making for a very short interview.

3. Plead ignorance:

Interviewers are impressed with people who know about the business they're involved in. So, if asked what you know, say, "Nothing," followed by, "What do you guys do here anyway?"

4. Downplay your skills:

Interviews allow employers to find out how your skills can benefit them. When the question comes up, say, "Gee, I don't know. I figured I'd just wing it and learn on the job?"

5. Your big chance:

At the end interview process you'll be given the opportunity to briefly summarize why they should hire you over other candidates. If you've made it this far, and you shouldn't have if you've followed my advice, it's your last chance to sell, or in your case, sink yourself. When the question, "Why should we hire you?" comes up, take a few seconds, pick your nose while you think about it, then say, "Hey, your guess is as good as mine".

FINAL THOUGHTS

If you followed the five steps and were hired anyway there is only one thing I can now say to you - Good luck with your new career as a telemarketer.

The Jerk At Work

How does someone with the interpersonal skills of thresher shark wind up in a position of authority over humans, a species with which they are obviously unfamiliar?

Yet, there they are, making life miserable for those forced to work with them, or around them.

They are the jerks at work.

My buddy Chester had to work so far around his boss, he'd end up in another dimension.

"This guy fires people to prove he's tough," Chester said. "Last Christmas eve he canned Harry, a guy with 17 years in the company, because his figures for the previous month were half the usual. You know why Harry's production was down? He'd been on vacation for three weeks."

"Jeez, how do you work with a guy like that?"

"You don't. You get rid of him."

"What with? Cement shoes?"

"A book. Guerrilla Office Tactics For The Corporate Jungle."

"Uzi included?"

"Nothing so crude. First step, organize. It was easy to recruit. This is a hated man."

"No doubt. So, what then?"

"Call the switch board and leave him messages."

"What kind of messages?"

"Test results for communicable disease's, threats of car repossessions, warnings from bookies about unpaid bets, reminders to attend meetings of left wing political parties . . . ."

"What'll that accomplish?"

"Lots. Once unleashed into the grapevine, rumors will mutate and grow like an unchecked bacteria. By the time they get to his boss, he'll sound like a herpes-infested deadbeat on skid row, who's sought by a contract killer and soliciting from clients for his bid as leader of the Peoples Popular Communist Front."

"Gee, that'll project a good corporate image."

"Then we leave incriminating memos, cover letters seeking employment elsewhere, judicial pardon request and membership applications for racist organizations, all implicating him on the photocopier nearest his boss's office."

"Why there?"

"So his boss will find them."

"What if his boss's secretary finds them?"

"Who do you think plants them there in the first place?"

"Oh, I see."

"Yep, we had everything ready to go. Then we had to scrap the whole plan."

"Scrap it! What for? Sounds like it could've worked."

"Sure it would have. But his boss discovered something else."

"What's that?"

"Besides being the biggest jerk, he was also the most incompetent. So she fired him."

The Complaint Department

My cousin Phil works in a complaint department. I dropped by one day to take him to lunch and while he was getting his coat in the back, the phone rang. So I thought, "what the heck, I'll just put it on hold," and I answered it.

"Complaint department, can you please . . ."

"Now don't you put me on hold," ordered the voice." I hate being put on hold. I've got a few complaints."

That made sense, because after all, this was the complaint department.

"There's nothing worse than being put on hold and having to listen to music not fit for an elevator."

"I know what you mean." I confided.

"Especially one with an annoying mechanical voice that cuts in every 30 seconds to tell you you're better off hanging on than hanging up and calling back, otherwise they might never get to you."

"Uh huh."

"I don't like that shopping cart system either."

"Shopping cart system?"

"Make me stick two bits in the dang thing so I'll put it back when I'm done."

"But you get your quarter back." I pointed out.

"The guy that thought up that system must be the biggest control freak in the world. Every day he forces millions of people to do exactly what he wants them to. I hope he rots in hell!"

"Gee, anything else?"

"Yeah. Barking dogs."

"Say, what?"

"Every one of my neighbors has got a barking dog. Yapping little one to great big woofers. I can't even think straight at times."

Like now for instance?

"And them little punks hanging around until three and four in the morning smoking dope, drinking, and swearing their heads off. Their parents should be strung up."

"Uh . . ."

"And when you're trying to watch two TV shows at a time, they synchronize the commercials just so you can't."

"Uh . ."

And then there's those morons who keep driving straight with their turn signals going. I just want to drive up beside them, roll down my window, point a shotgun at them, and . . ."

I pushed hold and slammed down the receiver.

Phil came out of the back, took one look at me and said, "You answered the phone, didn't you?"

"Uh huh."

"You idiot. This is the complaint department. Never answer the phone!"

"He . . . he had a whole list of complaints."

"They all do," said Phil, putting a comforting arm on my shoulder. "They all do."

Higher Education?

I was dropping my kids off at school the other day, when I ran into my old teacher, Mr. Dambrook. He's one tough old buzzard. We used to call him the Old Man and the C's. Albert Einstein couldn't salvage a B- in this guy's class.

He must be 106 and much to my surprise he was still breathing. But, as usual, most of it was hot air.

After giving me a late slip and a detention, just for old time's sake, he hitched his thumbs in his suspenders and pontificated. "We could make our education system the envy of the modern world. Plus end many of our daycare problems at the same time."

"Really?" I asked. "How's that?"

"First, we need to have a national standard."

Well, that'll give us one more thing to blame on the feds.

"Students from across the country will learn the same thing at the same time."

Yeah, but Eastern, Mountain or Pacific?

"Children are more sophisticated than they used to be," he continued.

"So my kids are at a higher level than I was then?"

"They're on a higher level than you are now."

You gotta love him.

"There's more to learn these days. I'd start them in pre-school at age three and extend the grades up to 16. That would put a student out of school at age 20."

So, instead of recess they'd have Miller time?

"We'd begin at 8:00 a.m. and go until 5:00 p.m. thus ending the daycare problem."

Parents'll love it. But the Kids? I hope his life insurance is paid up. "They'll sure be ready for summer vacation come June," I said.

"No two month summer holidays in this system," he opined.

"Are you serious?" Forget insurance. How about body armor?

"We'll go year round, with a four week floating vacation. Japan has a similar system with a Monday-to-Saturday school week. Look where Japan is today."

Asia?

"A six-day-school week is just what we need if we want to compete in today's high-tech world."

Well, maybe he had something. When I got out of high school there were tons of things I didn't know. Like what I was going to do with the rest of my life.

"You've got a lot of ideas, Mr. Dambrook. But aren't you just making more work for yourself?"

"It's no chalk off my board."

"Why's that?"

"I'm retiring."

Read On Mcduff

The first thing I do when I go to someone's house for an evening, someone I don't know very well, is go to the bathroom.

No, not for that. I check out their reading material.

You can tell a lot about a person by what he or she reads. You've heard the saying, "you are what you eat?" Well, I figure you are what you read as well.

For instance in my bathroom you'll find Writer's Digest, The Hockey News, an old Mad magazine, and a Kurt Vonnegut novel.

So, my reading material suggests I'm interested in writing, hockey, and satirical humor.

Now, what if you went to someone's house and found The National Law Journal, PC World, and Today's Christian Parent? If it were me, I'd avoid the lawyer and go play computer games with the kids.

How about these: Muscle And Fitness, Box-office Magazine, and Audubon Magazine. Okay, don't smoke, don't criticize Arnold Sshwartzenegger's acting, and for goodness sakes don't tell them you own shares in Exxon.

Now here's a situation I ran into.

I was at a friend of my wife's for dinner. I didn't know her or her husband, so I slipped into the washroom to reconnoiter and found the largest collection of Sports Illustrated I'd ever seen.

"No sweat," I thought. "The guys a sports nut." Out I

went.

"So," I said to Walter, "do you think Boggs will have a bad season after his little controversy?"

"I don't know. Who's Boggs?"

"He's a baseball player," I replied, somewhat confused.

"Oh," said Walter. "I really don't follow baseball." and he clammed up.

Hmmmm, picked the wrong sport did I? I waited awhile and tried again.

"Say, Walter, do you think San Francisco and Montana can pull it off again this year?"

"San Francisco isn't in Montana. It's in California."

"No, no, the San Francisco 49ers and Joe Montana, their quarterback."

"Oh, I see. That's football, right?"

"Uh, right."

"I never watch football." Again he sat silent, listening to our wives' conversation.

One last shot, hockey.

"What do you think about that trade situation between Vancouver and St. Louis?"

"That's very interesting," he said.

Finally I've got something here.

"But I think Vancouver's best opportunities for trade lie within the Pacific rim."

"Hold on a second here." I said.

"What?" asked Walter.

"I've been trying to discuss sports with you for the past hour. What sports are you interested in?"

"Quite frankly, I don't have any interest in sports."

"Then why do you have a zillion Sports Illustrated in your bathroom?"

"Oh, those. My Aunt gives me a subscription for

Christmas every year. I put them in there to keep them out of the way."

And another brilliant theory shot down in flames.

Goons Are Us

I love to play hockey. The first time I played I was hooked, literally! You see, I'm a little quicker on my skates than most, so I get hooked, slashed, speared, tripped, even punched during a game. I wouldn't mind so much if I was playing on a professional or competitive level. Thing is, I play for fun. Pretty radical concept, huh?

Sure, I could grab the nimrod who's trying to gaff me like a salmon and punch his lights out; being 6'2" and 210 lbs. has its advantages. But what for? It's only a game, right?

Try telling that to the Cro-Magnon's I play with. Like two clones I face off against every Friday night, the Barbarian brothers, Hack and Wack. I knew these guys were trouble the first time I saw them feloniously assault someone with intent to commit bodily harm. Call it a feeling.

One of my players was felled like a redwood by Hack, so he asked to see a current International Woodworkers Association membership card. Hack replied, by dropping his gloves.

Before you could say, "hoop around a barrel", his brother, Wack, had his gloves off and started pounding the closest guy to him. Sure it was his own goaltender, but what the heck, it's hockey, right?

Last week, our game was almost over, the clock ticking down through the final minute. Time for one last rush. I took a pass at center, turned on the jets and came in on the defense. It was Wack. I cut into the boards and had him beat, until he grabbed my arm. Just before it came off, he lost his grip, my arm came up, and brushed his pug-like face. Next thing I knew I was lying on the ice, crosschecked from behind.

"Don't touch me!" said Wack, standing over me.

"Say what?" I asked, incredulous.

"Touch me again, I'll kill ya'!"

I stood up in front of him. "You're not normal, are you?"

He crosschecked me again

"Shut your face!"

"Now hold on," I said, "I just want to get the rules straight here. Now it's okay for you to rip my arm out of my socket, but if I touch you, you'll kill me. Is that about right?"

"I'll smash your face!" he said, slashing me across the shinpads.

"But if you grab me, technically I'll be touching you. Now, will you kill me under those circumstances or does the judgment have to be qualified by which party initiates contact?"

Wack crosschecked me again. He was seething. "Shut you're face."

The Zamboni driver opened the gates, our time was up.

Hack skated up behind Wack and taped him on the shoulder. Wack, now fully pumped, dropped his gloves and turned around swinging. He got in one punch before Hack dropped his gloves. Blood and fists were flying. The two brothers were going toe-to-toe, eyes closed, swinging away. Everyone else on the ice, including me, moved back.

"Hey!" Shouted the Zamboni driver, "I'm calling 911"

"If you do," I shouted back, "you better tell 'em to send the goon squad."

Teed Off

I recently volunteered my services for a celebrity slave auction to raise money for charity. I was hoping to be purchased by an attractive young socialite for some sort of domestic duty. Unfortunately I was bought by Cosmo J. Farthing, a rotund, older gentleman whose size was only exceeded by his inflated opinions of himself.

He had me for the day. After I'd washed his Rolls Royce, cleaned his pool, manicured his hedges, cut his front lawn -- all 12 acres of it -- swept his chimney, and polished his silver, he decided it was time for a round of golf.

"Great idea," I said. "But I don't have my clubs."

"You won't need them," he said.

"I won't?"

"No. You'll be too busy carrying mine."

He had a private, nine-hole course on the back forty. On the first tee he drove the ball like a missile. A SCUD missile. Only he was twice as loud and half as accurate.

"Well? Don't just stand there," he said. "Find it!"

I was about to send back for supplies when I finally spotted his ball in the rough.

"What club should I use to get that back to the fairway?"

he asked.

"How about the explorer's club," I replied.

By the time he sank the putt I'd lost count of his score.

"Mark me down a five," he said.

"Oh! So we're dividing by three now are we?"

"Caddie, you're driving me to distraction!"

"Not if there's a pin near it."

As we approached the fourth hole, he'd dropped a few strokes, and I thought I was going to have one.

"So, what do you think of my game so far?"

"It's not bad," I said. "But I still prefer golf."

By the time we hit the seventh hole, the course behind us looked like an archeological dig. I'd seen less dirt fly at tractor pulls.

"So, where did you make all your money?" I asked.

"I accumulated vast amounts of real estate," he replied.

Probably saved his divots.

"It was a lot of hard work," he said. "I pushed myself too hard at times and endangered my health."

"Really?"

"Yes. Three years ago, my physician said I couldn't golf."

"So, he's played you then?"

On the eighth hole he had managed to get his ball on the wrong side of a water trap. He over-judged the distance and under-judged his skill and -- SPLUNK! -- in it went.

All I could do was shake my head.

"Well if you know so much about golf, how would you have played that last shot?"

"Under an assumed name," I replied.

"You are, without doubt, the worlds worst caddie!"

"No, sir," I said. "That would be too much of a coincidence."

It Ain't Over 'Til It's Over

Someday if I'm quoted, I hope I'm quoted like Oscar Wild and Dorothy Parker and not like Yogi Berra.

Yogi's a nice guy and all, but his quotes aren't exactly what you'd call full of wit or wisdom.

For instance, here are some familiar Oscar Wilde quotes.

On life's lessons: "Experience is the name everyone gives their mistakes."

Diversions: "Simple pleasures are the last refuge of the complex."

Skeptics: "What is a cynic? A man who knows the price of everything, and the value of nothing."

Human condition: "The world is a stage, but the play is badly cast."

Dorothy Parker wasn't quite as eloquent as Oscar Wilde, but what she lacked in elegance she made up for in the sharpness of her bite.

Asked to use the word horticulture in a sentence, she instantly came back with: "You can lead a whore to culture, but you can't make her think."

Ivy League Universities: "If all the girls who attended the Yale prom were laid end-to-end, I wouldn't be surprised."

Reviewing Katherine Hepburn in a play: "She runs the gamut of emotions from A to B."

Admonishing a drunk who insisted he had talent:

"Look at him, a rhinestone in the rough."

Describing a party she had attended: "One more drink and I'd have been under the host."

Yogi Berra, however, is in a class by himself.

On golf: "Ninety percent of putts that are short don't go in."

After watching a Steve McQueen movie: "He must of made that before he died."

After someone said he looked, nice and cool: "You don't look so hot yourself."

On baseball: "Baseball is 90 percent physical; the other half is mental."

Facing decisions: "When you come to that fork in the road, take it."

On life: "You can see a lot just by observing."

When asked for the time: "Do you mean now?"

Asked if he wanted his pizza cut into four or eight pieces: "Four. I don't think I can eat eight."

On personal habits: "I usually take a two-hour nap from one to four."

The position of the sun in the ballpark: "It gets late early out there."

On the economy: "A nickel isn't worth a dime any-more."

Dorothy Parker said, "I never seek to take the credit; we all assume Oscar said it."

So if you come across something I've written and you wonder what I've been smoking, remember; it couldn't possibly be me. You've read it before, Yogi's to blame. It's deja vu all over again.

Okay, it's over now.

Cream's Not The Only Thing That Rises...

It seems that Eric Lindros has finally been accepted into the NHL fraternity, after being appointed as assistant captain of Team Canada for the 1996 Canada Cup. But I haven't forgotten the controversy when he was first drafted or trying to explain back then to my buddy, Chester, what the Lindros vs. Quebec fuss was all about.

Chester, who's from California, wasn't quite up to speed on hockey culture. Being the expert that I am he turned to me for answers.

Unfortunately, my answers left him with more questions.

"Let me get this straight," he said. "This kid, Lindros, who dominated in junior hockey because he basically bullied a lot of smaller kids, gets drafted by the NHL. Then he acts like a classless idiot, ignoring tradition by not donning the jersey of his draft team, thus spitting in the eye of professional hockey?"

Well, it wasn't as bad as the Roberto Alomar thing as far as the spitting goes, but I think he got the general idea.

"You saw this eye-spitting thing on television?"

"Uh, metaphorically speaking."

"What was this, Lifestyles Of The Rude And Obtuse?"

"The Sports Channel, actually."

"His parents must be so ashamed?"

"No, I think they encouraged it."

"It's upbringing then? Or a mutated gene. He is kind'a big for his age."

"Maybe his book offers some insight," I suggested.

"His what?" Chester finally asked, after a stunned silence. "What is it, some sort of penitence thing for being such a selfish, arrogant little schmendrick?"

"Uh, no, not exactly."

"Well, what is it, a biography?"

I nodded and again a stunned silence.

"What has an 18-year-old kid possibly done that's so incredible he feels the need to share with the rest of the world? Was he raised by wolves? Taken to the planet Tralphaldamore for spectral analysis? Come on! As if no one's ever played junior hockey or been drafted by the NHL before?"

I shrugged. "I haven't read it."

"What's this thing called, Vanity and Self-exaltation Made Easy? How about, Zen And The Art Of Macro Conceit? My Attitude And Welcome To It, maybe? Or perhaps, How To Capitalize On God's Gifts And Take All The Credit?

"It's called Fire and Ice."

"Oh that explains it," he said.

"Explains what?"

"Well, fire and ice would produce steam, right? So I guess he's got a swelled head 'cause it's filled with all that hot air."

Rhyme And Reason

I found an interesting book in the library the other day. It's the Encyclopedia Of Associations. If you want to find a place to belong, that's where to look.

Curious, I skimmed through to see if there was something I might fit into. Maybe some sort of elite organization for writers like myself. Something like, The Association of Starving Humorists, or Satirist For a Stupid-Free Environment.

Satirist are like dentist; we're always trying to put ourselves out of business. When the world stops being a loony place, I'll stop writing. Not that I'm trying to give you incentive or anything.

I turned to writer's organizations and found Authors' Associations, Federations Of Writers, an Island Writers' Association (I guess they just write about islands. How exciting), and The League of Poets.

I was intrigued by that one. Imagine a league strictly for poets. Was it a seasonal league or a year round umbrella organization? What sports do poets play? Surely it would be something with rhythm.

Basketball has rhythm. You can hear it when the ball hits the floor, Thump duh-duh Thump duh-duh thump duh-duh Thump.

That might appeal to a poet. Sure! Giant men, floating through the air, stuffing the pumpkin colored ball through the hoop to the cheers of thousands. That has rhythm and pattern. It would go:

Thump duh-duh thump duh-duh thump duh-duh

float, stuff, cheer!

Well, maybe not.

How about baseball. That could appeal to a poet. It's a game that can suddenly explode into quick intense action. And it's full of colorful phrases like, "a swing and a miss", "the crack of the bat", and "good-bye, Mr. Spalding."

Golf is perfect for poets. A gentle and sophisticated sport in a serene setting, they could stand in the gallery during tournaments espousing verse.

"Nicklaus stroked his iron clean.

For an eagle it did sore.

Alas, it hit the grainy sand.

He bogeyed for a four."

How about hockey? Now there's a poets' sport. Even a beer commercial describes it poetically as "a quick silver ballet." How proper it would be for a poet to play a game so often described as "poetry in motion." That had to be it. What else would a poet play but hockey? I could really go for that. Margaret Atwood would be no match for me in a race for the puck. So I called them up.

"Say," I asked, "how does one get into the League?"

"Well," said the voice on the phone. "In case you didn't know it, you have to be a poet."

Damned elitists.

Holidays Are No Vacation

Remember that American Express commercial where a couple decide to just 'go for it' while on vacation? All they've got are the clothes on their backs until out comes the magical card. Suddenly they're in some tropical paradise buying everything from Bermuda shorts to banana plantations because -- membership has its privileges.

Back in the real world, I can't even get an American Express card.

No, vacations for me are a little different. I have to take everything with me, including my accommodations. The day before we leave, my wife and I pack two weeks worth of living into an 8 X 6 tent trailer for two wonderful weeks at the elegant Chateau La Tow.

It never fails. We'll be on the road three hours and realize something very essential was forgotten at home. I was determined not to let that happen again.

A month before, we started our list. As we packed, we checked it off.

"Okay," said my wife, "I'll check 'em, you pack 'em."

"Roger."

"Who's Roger?"

"No, it means . . . oh forget it."

"Pillows."

"Check."

"Sleeping bags."

"We're bringing your sisters?"

"Do you want to go alone?"

Hmmmm, a mind reader.

"Camera."

"Forget the camera, I always get stuck taking the pictures and never get in any."

"We want to see where we've been."

"That's what God created post cards for. Next."

"Your Walkman."

"You mean Loungeman don't you? I plan to do a heck of a lot more lounging than walking."

"Right. Camp stove."

"Check."

"Lantern."

"Check."

"First aid kit."

"Beer cooler's already in."

"What about bandages?"

"You only use them if the beer doesn't work."

"Matt's potty."

"What! Why can't he use the outhouse like everyone else?"

"He's to little. He might fall in."

"I'll bring my fishing rod."

"With your great skill we'd get him out just in time for college."

"Next!"

We finished at midnight. I slept restlessly. Not because I was excited about our trip, but because we packed the darn pillows in the trailer.

We got up, had a leisurely breakfast, climbed into the mini-van, and took off for parts unknown. Well, unknown to us anyway.

About three hours out, the car needed gas, and the

kids needed a bathroom, so I pulled into a service station. Full service of course, after all, I was on vacation.

"Fill'er up, son," I said.

"Check your oil, sir?"

"Good idea. And maybe check the tire pressure on the trailer while you're at it."

"Trailer? What trailer?"

I knew I'd forget something.

Things That Go Bump In The Night

Halloween is really for kids. We enjoyed it as kids, but it's not the same as an adult. The things that used to scare us don't anymore. That's not to say there isn't anything grown-ups are afraid of. Believe me. There is. So I offer the following verse for adults, about the things that we find scary on Halloween. I call it:

THINGS THAT GO BUMP IN THE NIGHT
Gather 'round and you will hear
'bout
Things that go bump
in the night.
Look towards the dark, there lies your fears
of
things that go bump
in the night.
Broom riding witches, vexing and hexing
Black cats, fur raised and hissing
A phantom rider, his head missing.
All the while Jack-o'-lanterns smile
at
Things that go bump
in the night.
Now they're stalking, at your door knocking
it's the

Things that go bump
in the night.
Of tricks beware, with treats be fair
with the
Things that go bump
in the night.
Pirates and clowns, ghosts with frowns
In search of suckers, Ju Jubes and Mounds
You fear there's not enough to go 'round
for the
Things that go bump
in the night.
And all the while Jack-o'-lanterns smile
at
things that go bump
in the night.
Now it's late, tucked away in your bed
from
Things that go bump
in the night.
Suddenly a sound that fills you with dread
of
Things that go bump
in the night.
The door creeks open, you start to shake
The screaming and wailing, you know is not fake
Because your little goblin has a tummy ache.
And all the while Jack-o'-lanterns smile
at
Things that go bump
in the night.
And when the sun rises in morning at dawn
You find they used toilet paper

to cover you lawn
and your little goblin kept you up all night long.
And all the while Jack-o'-lanterns smile
at
Things that go thump
Things that go clump
Things that go bump
in the night.
Happy Halloween folks. Oh, and please, for your own sake, don't forget the Pepto.

What's Red And White
And Malled All Over?

My Uncle Nick is Santa Claus. No, not the real Santa Claus. He's a mall Santa.

His elf, Sparky, had to go for a root canal, so he asked me to fill in. No Biggy. I mean, how hard could it be?

Then I saw the screaming horde of little darlings whining for the chance to vent their greed on Santa's lap.

Suddenly a root canal sounded pretty inviting. But I donned the green elf suit and took my place as chief of kiddy crowd control.

Part of my job was to get the kids' name to Nick without the kids knowing. He said it gave the illusion "Santa" had magic power.

These kids didn't care if he had nuclear power as long as he promised to deliver the goods Christmas morning.

"Hello, Timmy. What would you like from Santa?" Nick asked.

"I want a Creepy Crawler Moulding Oven, a Biker Mice from Mars Radical Rocket Sled, a Klingon Attack Cruiser, a Power Ranger Thunder Bike, and a . . . ."

"Ho, ho, ho. Anymore for you and Rudolph won't get my sleigh off the ground. Ho, ho, ho."

We were about ready for lunch when a little girl slipped by me and jumped up on Nick's lap.

"What does Sarah want for Christmas this year?"

"If it's okay, I'd like to ask for something for someone else?"

"Well, I suppose that's all right."

"It's my friend, Karen. She doesn't have a Dad. Her Mom has two jobs and works all the time. Karen hardly ever sees her."

"Goodness!

"Karen's Mom said you won't be visiting her this year."

"Really! Why?"

"She said parents are suppose to help Santa pay for their kids' toys, because you've got so many children to give presents to. But she can't afford it this year."

"Oh. I see."

"So could you give my present to her? I think she needs it more than I do."

A tear ran down Nick's rosy cheek. "All right, Sarah. I can arrange that."

"Oh, thank you, Santa!" And she gave him a big hug.

"Here's her address, just so you don't get mixed up. There's a lot of Karens you know."

"I know," said Nick softly.

She hopped down and disappeared into the throng of shoppers.

He looked at me over his round-wire glasses. "Every once in a while a kid like that comes along and makes being Santa a truly magical experience."

I had to admit, I was touched. I hate it when my disillusions are shattered

"Say, what would you have done if she hadn't had the address for you?" I asked.

"Oh, I have my ways."

Quite a guy my Uncle Nick.

Come to think of it, I didn't tell him her name was

Sarah.

How did he . . . ?
You don't suppose . . . ?
Naaaaa!

Noel

Being a volunteer firefighter means when the pager goes off, you go, whether it's Christmas Eve or not. And wouldn't you know it, that's exactly what happened.

BEEP! BEEP! BEEP! BEEP! *Hall four, hall four, we have a report of a man trapped at 555 Holly Lane. Jaws required."*

I stuffed myself into my pants. "It's three o'clock in the morning. Just great! Some drunk's put his car in a ditch on Christmas eve. Perfect!"

The chief had the rescue truck ready as I pulled in. I fired on my gear and we took off code three. But as we approached the scene, there was no accident in sight.

We pulled into the driveway. A woman ran up the walk. "Oh, thank goodness you're here. It's my husband, Noel."

"Fine ma'am," said the chief. "Now, where's the car?"

"Car? No, no! He's stuck in the chimney!"

"Where?" I asked.

"The chimney," she replied somewhat sheepishly. "I knew there'd be trouble when he bought that Santa suit."

"How you doing?" I called up the chimney, once inside.

"Oh my, my, my. I'm stuck, no doubt about it."

"Don't worry, we'll have you out in a few minutes."

"Please hurry. I've so many toys to deliver."

Noel's wife rolled her eyes and went to the kitchen to make coffee.

"No wonder he's stuck," said the chief. "He was tight

before he crawled in."

Ten minutes and three pounds of butter later we had him out. A plump little man in Santa suit with a huge sack stuffed full.

"Thank you. I knew this would happen eventually," said our victim, no worse for wear.

"Do this often, do ya'?" asked the Chief, wiping butter off his hands.

"Only once a year. I'm either getting bigger, or the chimneys are getting smaller, ho, ho, ho. Maybe I shouldn't have had that last egg nog," he said, stuffing boxes under the tree.

"I'd say that's a safe bet," said the chief.

All of a sudden, in the blink of an eye, he held a finger up to his nose, and with a wink, shot back up the chimney. "Merry Christmas to all, and to all a goodnight!"

"NO, WAIT!" We dove after him. Too late. Up he went.

"He gets stuck a'gin he's gonna stay stuck," the chief declared.

Just then, the front door swung open and in swayed a very drunk and very skinny Santa. "Merry Chrishmath!" he slurred.

"Noel?" asked the woman, returning from the kitchen.

"You were expecting Saint Nicholas maybe?" he asked.

The chief and I looked at each other.

"Are you thinking what I'm thinking?" he asked.

We looked at Noel swaying back and forth at the front door.

"Hey! said Noel, noticing us for the first time. "What's the matter with you guys? You never seen Santa Claus before?"

Just What I Wanted

Giving is what Christmas is all about, but c'mon! Add up all the friends, relatives, and colleagues on my list and we're talking major debt load here!

While my generosity knows no bounds, my credit limit is another story. I figured one more Yule-tide season and I'd need a second mortgage.

Finally, my fabulously frugal wife devised a plan to save us from financial ruin. I don't call her the accountant for nothing.

"You want to do what?" I asked.

"Draw names," she replied.

"How many names do I draw?"

"Just one. You still buy for the kids, and for me of course . . ."

What an optimist.

". . . But you'd only have to buy for one other."

"Does that mean I only get one present back in return?"

"You got it."

Good! I've got enough after-shave to fill a toxic waste dump.

Why do people always get gifts they have no use for? It would be nice to give someone something they actually wanted. That would be really special.

I was hoping for new skates, but they were too expensive. Even I couldn't buy them. Every time I asked the ac-

countant if we could squeeze them into the budget it was,
"no". Maybe I should stop asking her in bed. "No", seems to
be a conditioned response there.

The rest of the family agreed to the idea. We drew
names, set a $75 limit and nobody knew who had who,
until we gathered at my house Christmas morning. Lucky
me.

We let the kids open theirs first, as if we had a choice,
then one by one, we opened ours. After each package was
opened, the gift-giver revealed who they were. Finally,
there was one box left. My wife pulled it out. "It's for
Brock."

"For me? You shouldn't have."

"Open the gawl-darn thing so we can have some
beers," said Uncle Jake. He just wanted to try out his new
quart-sized mug.

I opened the box and pulled out a brand new pair of
kevlar-coated, CCM Super Tacks.

"Wow, this is great!" I exclaimed.

"Hey!" cried Uncle Jake. "What gives? You guys said
there's a $75 limit."

"Okay, who drew Brock?" asked my wife, quite an-
noyed. Nobody owned up. "You people knew the rules!"
she continued. "There was suppose to be a $75 limit
and . . . ." Suddenly, that familiar look of suspicion grew
upon her face. Then her eyes lit up as if a light bulb clicked
on inside head . . . . Wait a minute. Wait just a minute! You
drew your own name, didn't you?"

Uh, oh.

"Well, if the truth be known, yes."

"You can't do that," she said.

"You never said that when we drew names." Saved by a
technicality

"I hope you're happy," said my wife.

"You bet I am."

"Because you finally got your skates?"

"No. Because I finally experienced to joy of giving someone just what they wanted."

Some Assembly Required

It as Christmas morning and the presents under the tree were ripped open in the usual ritual of frenzied enthusiasm. The kids got toys, my wife got and a robe, and I got tie I'd never wear.

Everything was as it should be.

Everything that is except the box my mother had sent from California for my daughter.

It was a big box. Too big to be something simple. It looked like trouble.

Grandparents can cause parental stress with gifts at the best of times. But at Christmas, they can be down right dangerous.

The suspicious package was finally brought forward, its wrapping torn away, and my worst fears confirmed.

Stenciled on the side of the plain, brown box were the words "SOME ASSEMBLY REQUIRED".

My breathing quickened. I felt the walls begin to close in. The room began to spin. Spots of light started flashing before my eyes.

My wife put a paper bag over my head. It didn't help my hyper-ventilation, but at least no one had to look at me

Then, to my horror my daughter dumped the contents. Hundreds of screws, nuts, bolts and assorted pieces of metal clattered onto the floor.

Three hours and twelve dollars for the metal-detector

rental later, I was reasonably sure I had found all the pieces.

I sat, head in hands staring at the pile.

"Well, are you going to put the thing together or what?" asked my wife.

"I thought I'd just do the 'or what' for a while."

"Where are the instructions?"

"Of course! The instructions. Now why didn't I think of that? Now, where did I see them?"

"You hid them, didn't you?"

"Hid them! Hid them? Why would I hide them?"

"Because, my clever but mechanically inept mate, if the instructions are lost, you'll have the excuse you need not to embarrass and frustrate yourself trying to put that pile of recycled beer cans together."

"Oh. Here they are," I said, reaching into my back pocket. "I guess I stuffed them in there and forgot."

"Uh, uh."

"Say, must be about time for lunch. How about . . . ."

"How about you get started on your little project." She snatched the paper out of my hand. "Now let's find the picture of the thing and get . . . ."

She stopped, turned them over, then back again.

"You," she said, "have got horseshoes up your butt."

"Huh?"

She handed back the instructions.

I looked. Turned them over and back again. A smile grew on my face. There was no diagram. The directions were in text only, written in Korean, which coincidentally happened to be one of the many languages I am not conversant in.

"I can't believe that," she said. "You sure got out of that one."

Yes, until I saw the look on my daughters face, that is.

"All right. Give me my tool kit. I'm not a moron. I'll figure it out."

Nine hours later an odd-looking but complete doll house sat ready for use. Sure there were a few extra pieces; but what the heck, it was together.

Later that day, my mom called. "How did Krissy like her present?" she asked.

"She's playing with it right now."

"She's playing with it?"

"Yeah, up in her room."

"Why would she be playing with a closet organizer."

A Hugh Of Blue

The Bruins were on the sports channel; live from the Ga-dens. I'd been ready for weeks. I'd even left a special request for munchies in my wife's daytimer. Since I make the meals in our house, I figured it was payback time.

The anthem had just started when she planted herself between me and my 28" Hitachi.

"Look at you!" she said. "Bruins hat, Bruins shirt, Bruins sweat pants. You even have Bruins laces in your Reeboks! Now this!"

"What?"

"You want Boston baked beans, Boston blue fish, and Boston cream pie to eat during the game? I'm very concerned."

"What? What?"

"What? This obsession! That's what! You've never even been to Boston."

Time to set the record straight.

"You want obsession? Check out Blue Hugh."

"Blue who?"

"Blue Hugh. A Guy I knew in high school. He was a big supporter of the school basketball team, the Blues. He started wearing blue, the school colors, to every game. Then one game he dyed his hair blue. Next game, he painted his face blue too. Until one day he showed up blue, head to toe."

"So?"

"There wasn't a game.

"Oh."

"You see, his obsession wasn't with the Blues anymore. It was the color blue. Everything he did had a connection with blue. He'd only wear blue. He'd only listen to the blues, unless it was Blue Oyster Cult or the Moody Blues, or songs like 'Summer Time Blues' or 'Behind Blue Eyes'. The only beer he'd drink was Labatts Blue and he'd only drink it at the Blue Boy Tavern. As for restaurants, he'd only eat the blue plate special at the Blue Horizon.

"He had a video tape collection of blue movies."

"That's sick," my wife said.

"It's not what you think. I'm talking movies with blue in the title, such as Blue Lagoon, The Blues Brothers, and Blue Velvet.

"Even his job was part of his obsession."

"What was he, a Tidy Bowl man?"

"Nope. He made blue prints."

"Oh brother."

"So you see, that's obsessive behavior. I'm just having a little fun."

"All right, you win. What do you want to drink with your Boston bluefish?"

"A pot of Earl Gray."

"Huh? What does that have to do with the Bruins?"

"What! You've never heard of the Boston tea party?"

Happy Birthday,
Mr. President

One day I got a call from a Brit, named Raleigh Pennbroke, who said he had a great story. I'm always looking for great stories; Lord knows I can't come up with my own. I reluctantly agreed to meet this fellow at a pish-posh restaurant downtown.

The maitre d' sat us at a table in the establishment's conservatory and Raleigh began to tell me about a shipwreck.

"I drifted in a small rubber raft for days, falling in and out of consciousness, until I found myself washed up on the shore of an island. I crawled out of the water and saw two pair of feet in the sand. I looked up and saw . . . guess who?"

"Who?" I asked.

"Marilyn Monroe and John F. Kennedy!"

"Really?" I said, closing my note pad. When he said he had a story I didn't think he meant a story. I thought he meant, you know, a news story.

"They looked pretty old. But it was them."

"Marilyn Monroe and John F. Kennedy?"

"Amazing isn't it?"

"To say the least." To say the most was unprintable.

"He called her Peanut and she called him Jack, but I knew it was them."

"I see." That would have been the tip off for me too. "And what exactly were Marilyn and JFK doing on this island paradise?"

"When I told them I knew who they were, they told me the whole story. They met and fell in love, then faked their deaths so they could live out their lives together away from all the public furor. Besides, with him being catholic, divorce was out of the question."

"Makes perfect sense to me. Oh, look at the time! Gosh, I've got an appointment to have my teeth cleaned."

"But you haven't heard everything!"

"I have now," I conceded, and sat back down.

"They took me back to a village and there were dozens of them."

"Marilyns and JFKs?"

"No! Other public figures who wanted an escape."

"All right," I said. "Who else?"

"Well, let's see. There was Jim Morrison, Bruce Lee, Jimmy Hoffa . . . "

"What!? Come on!"

"It's true. And there were more. They'd all been brought there by FADE OUT."

"Who?"

"FADE OUT. Famous And Distinguished Entering Obscurity Under Tragedy. It's an organization that assists public figures who don't want to be public any more."

This was starting to make the grassy knoll theory look pretty good. Even Oliver Stone was becoming believable.

"It was a drastic measure, but they said they were desperate people. Finally, I convinced them I wouldn't tell anyone about them if they helped me get off the island. So they flew me back."

"Don't tell me. The pilot was . . . ."

"That's right, Amelia Earhart. So do you want to buy my story?"

"Buy your story? Sorry, Raleigh. But I don't buy it for a second."

"No one believes me. He was right after all."

"Who's that? Kennedy?"

"No, no. Elvis."

It Staggers The Mind

When I was a young man, still in my teens, I looked forward to attending that be-all and end-all of male rituals -- the stag.

Now, barely into my thirties, as soon as I get a wedding invitation, I try to book myself solid every weekend prior, for fear I'll also be invited to what I now recognize as an excuse to regress several evolutionary steps.

I swear, every afternoon I've been able to drag myself out of bed after one of those ordeals, the first thought that penetrates the fog into the dull, thumping pulp which was once my brain is -- never again.

But I still go. Time after time.

I guess you could call it a sense of duty.

You see -- I've been through it before. I won't embarrass you with the details. Not that I can remember the details. Let's just say there was some detailing going on.

So now, I go with a definite purpose -- to look after the groom-to-be.

Most people who get married are quite young, at least the first time around. Their friends are quite young too. And it's their friends who throw the stag. In most cases, with little, if any experience in this all-important social custom. So they have a tendency to go a little overboard.

The summer my youngest brother got married, his best man asked me how things should be handled. A wise move on his part. Finally someone had enough sense to seek my advice. Finally we could dispense with adolescent shenanigans.

Sanity would prevail.

"Brock, buddy, what are some of the things you've experienced at stags?" he asked.

"Chip," I said, "you just wouldn't believe some of the things people have pulled."

"Yeah? Like what?"

"Well, I remember one time they got this guy drunk. Really drunk. They poured him into bed. Then they put three scantily clad women in with him and took polaroids."

"You're kidding!"

"No. Then as a joke, they sent the pictures to his fiancée by courier."

"Really?"

"Yeah. She called the wedding off."

"That's terrible."

"Yeah. Another time they forced the groom into women's clothes. We're talking bra, panties, panty hose, the works."

"No!"

"Yeah. Then they told him that for every shot of scotch he drank, he could take an article of clothing off. If he got it all off, he could put his own clothes back on."

"What happened?"

"He got down to the panties and passed out cold."

"More pictures?"

"Nope. They duct-taped him to a street lamp on the main drag."

"That's terrible."

"It gets worse."

"No, way! What could be worse than that?"

"Here's the worst."

"What?"

"Three days before the wedding they plied this guy with liquor, packed him in a box, and mailed him to the church."

"No!"

"Yeah."

"No!"

"Oh yeah."

"What happened?"

"You know the postal system."

"Wow. I can't believe it."

"Horrifying, isn't it?"

"Yeah. Which one should we do?"

A Recyclable Built For You

Do you know anyone who is fabulously wealthy? I do. Cosmo J. Farthing. His interest earnings are higher than the GNP of most third world nations.

Cosmo made his money the old fashioned way -- land exploitation.

Way back when, he started buying up land. People thought he was nuts. "Imagine," they said, "paying a hundred dollars an acre for that bush along the river. What's he gonna grow there?"

He grew houses. Lots and lots full of them.

Now there's not an open space left to pour a foundation. So, he sits up there on the hill, in his big old house with his wife, Penny, and his son, Buck, contemplating life and counting his money.

But idle time has a way of playing on the mind. And boy, did it play with his. After all, there was a lot of room in there.

I wandered into the local watering hole around Miller time and there was old Cosmo, sitting in a corner with half a bottle of brandy in a snifter.

"Hi, Cosmo," I said. "What's up?"

"The slings and arrows of outrageous fortune, my boy."

"Cheer up. Think about your Grand Canyon wave pool idea."

"It's no use. I've gone as far as I can go and done as

much as I can do."

"What makes you say that?" This from a man who phoned NASA to inquire about view property on the Sea of Tranquillity.

"This book," he said, tossing a paperback on the table.

"Recyclical Reincarnation?" I said, picking it up. "What's it about?"

"The book says, when you're reincarnated you don't come back as a different personality, but rather as yourself, with the same likes and dislikes, the same talents and abilities."

"Oh yeah? You mean you don't come back in your next life as a dog or a cow or something?"

"No you don't?"

"That's good." With my luck I'd come back as a goalie. Oh, the horror.

"Each time around you improve on your last incarnation until you've reached the highest level of your calling."

"Really? That sounds kind of far out." Actually it sounded really far out. "What do you mean by, improve?"

"After reading the book, I discovered that in my first life, I was a serf."

"You were a small blue elf?"

"No, that's a Smurf."

I knew that.

"I progressed from serf to renter, then from renter to rent collector until eventually, through a series of incarnations, I became the successful land developer you see before you."

"That's quite a concept, Cosmo." Gosh! Maybe Cosmo has gained some enlightenment here. Maybe next time it'll be parks instead of parkades, rolling hills instead of bankrolls. Poor guy's probably filled with regret. "So you're depressed about . . . ."

"That's right, lad. I'm upset about my next incarnation. Do you realize what an acre of land will be worth then?"

You know, some people will never learn.

What's In A Name

Names have a cultural significance.

Most of us know our last names have a meaning attached to them, their roots now well hidden beneath our family trees. Surnames in the British Isles, where mine originated, have four main categories; names based on first names, local origins, status or occupation, and finally nicknames.

It took centuries for these names to evolve into their modern usages. What one day was, "good day to you, one who makes barrels," is now, "hello, Mr. Cooper."

Did you also know our first names have meanings attached to them as well? I didn't realize this until we tried to find a name for our second child. We bought a book on first names and were surprised to see each had roots of their own. Then the notion struck me, what would it be like if we addressed each other by the root meanings instead of the evolved names? Hmmmm.

So here are a few common names you'll recognize. Let's try our little experiment at a cocktail party and listen in. I'll put the names we use now in brackets and the root meanings in italics. Ready? Okay, here we go.

"Hello, *Warlike One* (Mark). How's your wife, *Little Raven* (Brenda)?"

"Oh, hello, *Dweller of the Church* (Kirk). *Little Raven's* just great. How is *Helper and Defender of Mankind* (Sandra)?"

"She's fine, just fine. She's over there talking to *Belongs to Mars* (Marcia) and *Dweller of the Gray Fortress* (Leslie)."

"Uh, oh! Here comes *Invincible War Shield* (Randy). He made a pass at, *Son of the Dark One's* (Kerry) wife, *Pool Below a Waterfall* (Lynn) last time we were here.

"Did his wife, *One from the Meadow on the Ledge* (Shelley) find out?"

"You bet she did. She packed up their two kids, *Young Verdant* (Chloe) and *Noisy One* (Tristan) and moved in with her mother."

"You mean she's living with old, *Battle Maid* (Hilda)?"

"You got it. And I hear her father, *The Supplanter* (James) is none too happy about it."

"I guess not. They've still got their younger son at home. He must be 22 or 23 by now. What's his name again?"

"*One like a Dog* (Caleb)."

"Yeah, that's it. *One like a Dog*."

"So, you see any good movies lately?"

"Yeah! I Saw Dances With Wolves."

"What's that about, a tap dancing zookeeper?"

"No, it's about a guy who lives with Indians (indigenous Americans). That's the name they gave him."

"What! Dances With Wolves? What kind of stupid name is that?"

He Who Lives By The Sword

It was a dark and stormy night. I splashed through the convention center parking lot, drenched from the torrential, west-coast monsoon. The sign above the door, read Welcome to the 9th Annual Genre Writer's Convention. I followed the arrows down a corridor into the first room. People in small groups sipped brandy. I approached two men in conversation.

"Then she cut up the pieces," said one, "and dissolved them with acid in the bathtub."

"That's perfectly grisly," Commented the other.

"Thank you," replied the first.

Hmmmm. Mystery writers.

"Say," I said, "do you fellows know where the humorists are?"

"Haven't a clue," said one, "but I did detect the sound of mirth down the hall."

"That's right," said the other. "The evidence suggests that would be the direction to take."

"Thanks." I headed to the next room.

There was another group talking and sipping tea. I walked over to two women chatting.

" . . . Then he gently brushed her flowing blonde hair from her face," said one. "They embraced and kissed passionately as the sun slowly drifted below the horizon."

"Beautiful, simply breathtaking," said the other.

"And that's only the opening paragraph," said the first one.

"Excuse me, ladies," I said, "but do you happen to know where the humorists are?"

"Humorists are not very romantic," said one.

"They're just not serious enough," shot the other.

I took that as a no and tried the next room.

"Then Zargon, who was really the illegitimate son of Zombo, the evil ruler of the planet Tarnack, sabotaged the power inversion coil to the hyper drive engines, leaving the star-destroyer incapable of firing its deadly anti-matter particle-beam at the planet Palandrin," said one.

"Brilliant!" exclaimed another, as the rest murmured their approval.

"Live long and prosper," I said.

"Live long and prosper," they replied.

"My mission is to seek out humorists," I said, "to go where no Brock has been before."

"Humorists, you say?" said one.

"Humorists are not logical," offered another. "Perhaps a quadrant further down the hall."

The next room had a crowd of people smoking, drinking beer, hooting and guffawing. I walked up to the first person I saw.

"Humorists?" I asked.

"Through that door," he said.

Finally! "Great! Thanks a lot."

"Anytime," he said, chuckling.

I pushed it open, stepped through to hear it close and lock behind me. There I was, once again, in the pouring rain.

Hmmmm. I think I found them.

Early To Bed, Early To Rise: Advertise, Advertise, Advertise.

Okay. All those who've gone through the frustration of unemployment raise your hand.

Two, three, four . . . just about everybody, I thought so.

Well, then you can relate to my buddy Richy.

He's been trying to get into advertising. He'd graduated, looked for work, but hadn't found a thing. Which was surprising because this guy is really sharp.

One thing he does better than anyone is bulletproof his ads.

What's bulletproofing?

Well, it's writing your copy so it can't be turned around to ridicule. He explained it to me while venting his frustrations over a couple of beers.

"I can't understand it," he said. "Here I am, can't find a thing, and there are guys out there making big bucks writing ads you could fire a cannon ball through."

"What do you mean?" I asked.

"Their ads. They're not bulletproofed."

"Bulletproofed?"

"You bulletproof by writing your ad so it doesn't get turned around and work against you."

"Give me some examples."

"Okay. Look at car ads. Take Honda for instance. What's their slogan? 'We make it simple,' right? Now what does that say to you?"

"Just what it says. They make simple cars. Why, what does it say to you?"

"It says, 'We make it simple, because the people who buy our cars aren't too bright.' See what I mean?"

"Go on."

"Another one that bugs me, Nissan. Now listen to theirs. 'Cars made for the human race'."

"I think that's kind of clever."

"Yeah, real clever. Cars that are actually made for people. What a radical concept."

"Oh yeah, I see."

"Mazda, theirs kills me. 'It just feels right.' We don't have a clue how it works, but it feels right. But the one that gets me the most is Chrysler's campaign."

"What's wrong with theirs?"

"Now don't get me wrong I think Chrysler makes a good car. I think they all make good cars. But what's the hottest issue in the world today?"

"Russian hockey players in the NHL?"

"The environment."

"Oh right, I knew that."

"So what does Chrysler do? They showcase their vehicles in a hostile looking environment, see? No grass, no trees, nothing but dirt and rocks. And the slogan says, 'Chrysler, changing the landscape'. Now I don't know about you, but to me it says 'Our cars are changing our lush green planet into this barren looking place. So buy our cars and you too can be a part of the destruction of the planet as we know it."

"Thanks, Richy. Now I'm depressed."

"Why are you depressed? You've got a job."

"Sure, but I just traded my Pontiac in on a Chrysler mini van."

"Oh! Well I didn't' mean to . . . "

"Say, Richy, I notice you're wearing Reeboks."

"Yeah, so what?"

"Well, if Reeboks let you be you, who were you before?"

Bookworm

Hollis Crips' life ambition was to own a used bookstore. When he saw the ad reading 'Wanted: individual who loves books to work in used book store,' he might as well have won the lottery.

The bell above the door tinkled as he entered the shop. "I've come about the job," said Hollis.

"Like books do you?" asked Mr. Simmons, the proprietor.

"Love them," answered Hollis. "I aspire to own a shop like this myself one day."

"Good. Hang up your coat. I pay minimum wage." And Hollis began his career.

After a few of months, Simmons decided Hollis could run the store while he pursued his life ambition -- retirement.

Hollis was in heaven. He dusted shelves, alphabetized, categorized, and ran the store as if it was his own. There was one problem. It wasn't.

"I could have my own store," he thought. "If only I had enough books." Then he had an idea. When people traded in their old books he'd put a few aside and take them home. When he had enough, he'd open his own store. Soon Hollis' small apartment was overflowing, so he called Mr. Simmons.

"Quitting?" Simmons asked. "You tired of the book business already?"

Hollis, having pangs of guilt, didn't want Simmons to know about his new venture. So now, on top of everything else, he lied. "That's right. I guess I'm not cut out for it."

Simmons decided to close shop and gave all his books to the Salvation Army. "Too bad Hollis lost interest," he said to his wife. "I'd have given him the whole works to make up for his lousy wages."

Over the years, Hollis' book store did pretty well and he finally decided to hire some help and take a little time off. He placed an ad worded the same as the one Mr. Simmons had used years before. The following day the bell above the door tinkled and in walked a young man. "I'm here about the job."

"You like books?" asked Hollis.

"Love them. I'd even like to open my own bookstore one day."

Hollis smiled, thinking about a similar conversation he'd had. Then slowly, his smile faded.

"I'm sorry. The jobs no longer available."

The following day an ad appeared in the local paper. 'Wanted: individual who doesn't like books to work in used bookstore. Only those without aspirations need apply.'

How To Get Rid Of Your Neighbor

Old Dave Jenkins lived near the sea and next to a golf course.

His two favorite things in life, fishing and golf, were only a block away - Shangri-La!

Dave's yard, behind the eighth hole, offered an endless supply of free golf balls. Mornings he'd pick up a dozen worms, a half-dozen golf balls, and be set for the day.

Life was good. Then one day, Dave got a new neighbor.

"J. Thurbourne Pierce, Attorney," said Dave's new Neighbor thrusting a business card into Dave's open hand.

"Just what the world needs," muttered Dave, "another lawyer."

Soon the community felt the influence of its new member.

Attorney Pierce didn't like the way the Widow Jones' dog barked at strangers. So he went to court and had it muzzled. Within a week, her house was robbed.

Attorney Pierce, unlike everyone else, drove his prized 1953 MGTC roadster the full speed limit through the neighborhood. Since slowing down long enough for street-hockey players to scurry for cover took at least three seconds off his ETA, he had the local police put a stop to the sport.

Then it happened. Attorney Pierce didn't like stray golf balls in his yard, so he sued the course.

When Dave's supply of free golf balls ended abruptly as the greens keeper, under court order, moved the eighth hole, he came to the only conclusion possible. Attorney Pierce had to go.

Dave cast an eye at the automotive-ego-rub parked next door and decided to let nature do his work for him.

Within a few months the litigator's antique roadster disappeared for a week, only to return with a new paint job.

"Nice paint," said Dave.

"Should be for three grand!" said Attorney Pierce.

"How come?"

"Rust," said Attorney Pierce walking to his front door. "But the body shop took car of that."

"It's the salt air, you know?"

Attorney Pierce froze. "What do you mean?"

"Pacific ocean's down the block, Counselor. Salt air. It corrodes. Carport ain't no good. You need a place with a garage."

A few months later the roadster disappeared for another week and materialized with another new paint job.

"How much this time?" asked Dave.

"Five!" said Attorney Pierce, covering his car with a tarp."

"Won't work. Salt air penetrates everything. You need a place with a garage."

A few months later the roadster headed for the body shop and Attorney Pierce headed for the real estate office, looking for a house with a garage.

As Dave Jenkins and his wife watched the moving van pull away, she said, "It was a twenty-four-hour job putting up with that man."

"Yep," replied Dave, emptying the jug of salt water he had in his hand. "But, rust never sleeps."

Old Mrs. Winter

A wise and wonderful lady died recently, Mrs. Winter. She was 92. She lived two houses down from where I'd grown up. I'd known her since I was four. I learned a lot from her. She taught me magic; the magic of words. I'd go visit her and she'd always be waiting with a cup of tea, some scones and a book. Her house was filled with books. She loved books. She also had three grandchildren. I don't remember them ever visiting her. You could tell. If they had, they might've turned out different - human.

I arrived at the office of Riley J. Finnigan, attorney at law, after being informed at the funeral of my inclusion in the will. The grandchildren were already there. None had been at the service. Finnigan wore a stern look as he began to read.

"To Brock Macdonald, my former neighbor, I leave my books. May the richness between the pages bring him the wealth of wisdom."

I was stunned. It was as if she'd passed on to me her very soul, her spirit for safe keeping. A lump formed in my throat and my eyes began to cloud.

Arthur sighed in relief. Margaret put a hand to her mouth to hide a grin. Spike laughed out loud, leaned over and nudged me.

"You came all the way here for some books?" he said through a grin.

"I came to say good-bye to your grandmother," I replied.

"I think you're a little late, sport," he said, behind a smirk.

Finnigan cleared his throat and continued.

"To my granddaughter Margaret, I leave my vacuum, mop and cleaning supplies in hopes she'll clean up her act."

"What? That's it? A vacuum and spray cleaner?"

"Yes," said Finnigan.

"At least I didn't get stuck with a bunch of stupid, old books!" She looked at me, then fled the scene.

Finnigan read on.

"To my oddest grandson, Arthur . . . ."

"Shouldn't that be oldest?" interjected Arthur.

"No." Replied Finnigan.

"Oh."

"To my oddest grandson, Arthur, I leave all my clothes, since they were his only interest the few times he was in my house."

Arthur's face turned deep red. He got up and quickly left.

Spike sat forward, rubbing his hands together, looking as if he might salivate.

"And to my youngest grandson, Spike, I leave the bulk of my estate . . . ."

Spike jumped out of his chair.

"Oh yeah! I knew that call at Christmas would pay off. Thanks Finnigan. I'll get the details later. See ya', Brock, have a nice read," and he was out the door.

Finnigan had a shamrock-eating grin on his face as he looked at me over his glasses.

"What exactly did he get?" I asked.

"Why, the bulk of the estate, after taxes and a generous donation in the form of a new wing to the library, of course."

"Which leaves?"

Finnigan began again.

"And to my youngest grandson Spike I leave the bulk of my estate -- my lawn mower. He never used it while I was alive, maybe he'll get some use out of it now."

So, even though Mrs. Winter had gone, she left yet something else for me to ponder.

Thanks, Mrs. Winter. I'll miss you.

People Who Live In Glass Houses

Joe has a great house. Cedar paneling, hardwood floors, and the thing I like best, windows that stretch from the floor to the vaulted ceiling. There's glass everywhere. It's like a green house.

Yeah, I love Joe's house. Joe's attitude? Well . . . .

"I've had it with these guys, man!" he said to me when I was over one day.

"Can you narrow that down a bit?" I asked.

"You notice the lawn ornament next door?"

"You mean the small block Chevy?"

"Yeah, that's it."

"I take it he works on cars?"

"You kidding? Check out his driveway. He's spilled more oil than the Exxon Valdez!"

Joe opened a drawer in the table beside him, took out a baggy of pot and a some rolling papers.

"And," he continued, "he's got a rusty old beater about the size of a Trident submarine mothballed beside his house."

I looked out the wall of glass at Joe's new Mustang GT. "Not everyone can drive a new Ford, Joe."

"Are you kidding? That thing hasn't moved since Ford was in office."

Joe finished rolling a joint and stuck it in his mouth.

"There's bylaws for that kind of thing, you know." He struck a match, fired up and drew the smoke into his lungs before offering it to me.

I waved him off. "No thanks. Not into it."

He shrugged, exhaled, and took another hit.

"Then there's these new goofs across the street."

"What's their great sin?" I asked, looking at the house in question.

"You should see it. They've got five, count 'em, five, pieces of junk parked over there! They park three of 'em on the lawn! I fixed 'em though. Like I said. There's bylaws for that kind of thing."

"What did you do?"

"I reported 'em? Yeah, you bet your butt I did," he said, bringing the joint up to his lips again.

"Don't you think you could've maybe talked to them first?" I suggested.

"Forget it. They're scum. I'll let the law take care of them." He took another toke.

Finally, I had to say something.

"Joe, do you see something wrong with this picture?"

"What d' ya' mean?"

"In the big scheme of things, what's worse in terms of law breaking, parking on the grass, or smoking it?"

Joe's answer was interrupted by the doorbell.

"I'm officer Turnbull," said the cop when Joe opened the door.

"Good!" said Joe. "I guess you here about the junk dealers across the street, huh?"

"No, sir."

"No?" said Joe.

"Someone reported seeing a man smoking marijuana. Kind of hard to miss with those windows," he said. "I saw you half a block away." The cop sniffed the air. "Are you in possession of an illegal substance, sir?"

Joe got off with a hefty fine. I wonder if he learned anything from this lesson.

The lesson? People who live in glass houses shouldn't get stoned.

All The World's A Stage

It was the end-of-the-season party for the local community theater group and everyone was really down. It should have been a banner year, but they were thousands in the red. It looked like they might fold.

"Brock! Brock, you lovely boy!" It was Delores Garnet, the society's treasurer and perpetual bit-part understudy. "I must tell you about my upcoming trip." She grabbed my arm eliminating any chance of escape. "I leave tonight for La Grand Shakespearean festival of Argentina. I simply can't believe my good fortune. The travel agent said I booked the last spot on the tour. Oh, what a treat!"

"Gee, sounds great." I grinned and let her drone on. She'd talk for hours if someone was around to listen. Her husband died of a heart attack watching Lawrence Welk. She flapped her gums for two hours before she noticed he was dead.

She jabbed me in the ribs. "Brock, who's that man over there?"

I followed her gaze to some guy who made Orson Wells look like an aerobics instructor. Talk about stick out in a crowd. This guy was a crowd. Then I noticed he kept glancing over at us.

"I have no idea. Why? You looking to drag . . . I mean, take someone to Argentina?"

"Don't be preposterous."

"Why not? You've got the bucks."

"What?" She looked at me like I said her face was on fire.

"You've got no expenses, you sold your house last week, you should be rolling in dough."

"Stay out of other people's business," she said and bolted.

I made a mental note to bring up the subject of money next time she cornered me.

Then I heard a commotion in the kitchen. Delores was squealing above the din. Curiosity piqued, I went to investigate.

"LET GO!" she shouted at the fat man. He had one side of her big canvas bag; she had the other. Both were giving it all they had. A crowd formed behind me. Everybody likes a good brawl. You never know; a hockey game might break out.

"You want me to call the police or something?" I asked, thinking that would bring things to a halt.

"NO!" yelled Delores.

Chubby looked up, sweat pouring off his brow. "Call them! Call them NOW!"

"What do I say, that I wish to report a tug-a-war?"

The bag split and bills exploded into the air. Delores fell to her knees whimpering and scooping dead prime ministers and aged queens off the floor. "No. It's mine. It's mine."

No wonder the theater was broke.

"It's all right," said the fat man, flipping open a wallet to reveal a badge. "I'm a private investigator. Would someone please bring me a phone so I can call the police?"

Delores had a real odd expression.

"Better tell them to call the Waldorf Hysteria," I said. "I think she's going to need a reservation."

He looked down at her. "You're really not a very good embezzler, Mrs. Garnet."

"You think that's bad," I said, "you should see her act."

Portrait Of An Artist
As A Young Fraud

There I was, at another one of Marilyn Biscayne-Smythe's socials for the Mundane Society, or whatever it is they call themselves. You know the drill; upper-middle-class, upper-middle age, arts matrons with nothing better to do than eat sushi rolls, sip chardonnay and out spend one another.

On the other side of the room was the honored guest; a neo-impressionist named Randolph, or Excelsior or Fabio, or something. Marilyn found him and convinced the society to sponsor him. Sweet deal for him I suppose. He even has his studio in her house.

I don't know what the big deal is with this guy. I've seen his work. I swear he jumps buck naked into pails of paint then rolls around on the canvas. Nice work, if you can get it.

There's always three or four of the old girls orbiting around him, although Marilyn's usually in his lower atmosphere.

I'd had about all I could take of polite conversation, so I decided to find Marilyn and make my excuses. Someone said she'd gone up to Randolph's studio. Private sitting no doubt.

As I made my way to the stairs, Marilyn's husband, Warren, entered through the front door. He looked awful.

His face was gray with big black circles under his blood-shot eyes.

"Hello, Warren," I said. "I'm surprised to see you here."

"Huh?"

I almost gagged. He smelled like the top end of a half empty bottle of Jack Daniels.

"I thought you worked late when she had these things?" I said, weaving and bobbing away from his breath.

"Have you seen my wife?"

"I think she's in the studio."

He headed up the stairs.

"Say good-bye for me will you?"

I grabbed my coat and was half way out the door when I heard the beginning of an argument from upstairs.

"This sounds interesting." I went back in and stood by the landing with my ear cocked up the stairs. I soon heard the unmistakable smack of fist meeting face, followed by a thud, which I took for face meeting floor.

Warren trotted down the stairs, looking a little happier than when he went up, mumbling, ". . . I'm out of a job, he's out of a job."

I heard Marilyn sobbing in Randolph's studio. I went up and peeked in. There was Randolph, out cold, laying on a canvas, buck naked, covered in red, yellow, and blue paint.

See, I told you.

Nouveau Politolingo Americana

Politics is a dirty game. With all that fertilizer flying around it's no wonder. A few years ago some nasty rumors were floating around about one to the candidates in my town.

I just couldn't figure out how these rumors got started. That is, until the source knocked on my door.

"I'm canvassing for the re-election of Mayor McClease," said the bright-and-smiley face.

Mayor McCheese, as my daughter calls him. Or as I refer to him, Mayor McSleeze.

Why? How about three convictions under the consumer protection act? The guy owns a used car lot. Need I say more?

"May I explain the mayor's platform?"

Better explain it to the mayor first, I thought. Intellect to electricity, he was running at about 25 watts.

"Actually," I said, "I'm voting for his opponent."

"I think that would be a grave error sir. A person of his character could have an innocuous effect on the moral fiber of our community."

Innocuous? "What do you mean?" This, I had to hear.

"He's a well-known extrovert."

"No!"

"Oh, yes. It's a common fact he attempts social intercourse with everyone he meets."

"No!"

"Oh, yes. Everyone. Men, women, children, it doesn't seem to matter."

"Kids too?"

"Oh, yes. Just the other day, while at a children's party, he displayed illusory behavior with balloons shaped like animals."

"No!"

"Oh, Yes! There was even a photograph of him in the local newspaper masticating at a table full of small children."

"No!"

"Oh, yes. Of course, with his family background, what could you expect?"

"His family background?"

"His sister is a thespian, who's actually performed on stage."

"No!"

"Oh, yes. And that's not the half of it."

"There's more?"

"His brother is a practicing Homo Sapien who gesticulates while talking to others."

"No!"

"Oh, yes. So, as you can see, there's no telling what could happen if a man like that were elected."

"You're absolutely right."

"I'm glad you agree sir."

"Why, we can't have a mayor who likes people, actually talks to them, does magic tricks for children, chews his food, has an actress for a sister and a human being for a brother. I mean, that's almost as bad as having a perfidious improbitarian who rolls back odometers and hands fat, city contracts to friends and relatives. Sort of like the one we have now."

The face that was no longer bright-and-smiley said, "I guess this means we can't count on your support?"

"You know what?"

"What?

"That's the first honest thing you said."

From Primaries To Prime Suspect

It looks like my Uncle Brian has got himself in a bit of a jam now that he's retired from politics. Uncle Brian always said, Those representing the people should be intelligent, diligent, hardworking and honest. But he ran anyway.

The day he decided to run, Uncle Brian stole a hat, threw it in the ring, climbed the nearest soapbox and lied his face off.

The pundits said it was the fastest start they'd ever seen. "It usually takes a while in a political race to distance one's self from the truth," said one commentator. "In that sense he's light years ahead."

Although I must say, when he did stumble over the truth, he picked himself up, brushed himself off, and carried right on like nothing happened.

"Being a politician is a very promising career," Uncle Brian said. Promising, yes. But keeping the promises is an entirely different matter.

I wasn't sure how leaving politics would effect his ego, which is not what I'd consider a benign growth. To say he is overly aware of himself would be an understatement of microscopic proportions.

He even had a portrait of himself in his office.

It's wasn't a true resemblance though. You see his

mouth was shut and his hand was in his own pocket.

The artist totally missed two prevalent personality traits -- his gift of gab and gift of grab.

When it came to his gift of gab people didn't want to know the topic as much as they wanted to know the duration, so they can set the little wake-up alarms on their watches.

After all, four out of five doctors do recommend him for insomnia.

But when it came to his gift of grab it would seem it was one of his more hidden talents.

Hidden in a Swiss bank account that is.

But I like to think we can all learn from our mistakes. If we're fortunate, the lessons learned from Uncle Brian's term of office will be remembered by future generations. And the next time someone leaves public office and immediately drops $5 million cash on mansion, they'll remember to check the silverware in the Parliamentary dinning room.

And while I won't forget, I am willing in a way to forgive.

I'm even going to help out Uncle Brian in his future career.

You see, I'm going to order a personalized license plate. And when he presses the letters into that plate in his new place of employment at the Crowbar Hilton, he'll be the first to see a word I've been waiting to say in regards to dear, old, Uncle Brian for a long time.

"GOTCHA"

Wishful Thinking

What would you do if you found a magic genie? Wish for money, right?

Not me. Wishing for money shows a total lack of creativity.

I'd make one wish. The only wish I'd need.

What is it?

I'd say, "Genie, every time I make a suggestion starting with the phrase, *don't you think*, whoever listens will be compelled to take my advice."

You'd take the money?

Maybe I should elaborate.

Let's say I'm broke. I walk into the most popular restaurant in town, order the most expensive item on the menu, then say to the maitre 'd, "*Don't you think* this meal should be on the house?".

He listens and -- SHAZAM! Eat your heart out Diner's Club; lobster has just become an endangered species.

Now, I need a place to live.

No problem. I just say to a developer, "*Don't you think* you should build me a big house to live in free-of-charge?".

He listens and -- SHAZAM! I'm living high on the hog in a mansion high on the hill.

But wait! The driveway's empty!

No problem. I simply call my local Chrysler dealer and say, "*Don't you think* you should give me a new Viper?"

He listens and -- SHAZAM! I'm driving a sleek, street-smart snake.

I'd need a steady income, so I'd call up the publisher of the Washington Post and say, "*Don't you think* you should hire me as a columnist at $500,000 a year?"

He listens and -- SHAZAM! Suddenly I'm on the op-ed pages of one of the most prestigious dailies in the country and finally paid what I'm worth.

Gosh, what if I had nothing to do on Saturday night? No problem. I simply call the Yankees and say, "Gee, Mr. Steinbrenner, *don't you think you* should give a sky box and season tickets?"

He listens and -- SHAZAM! Next thing you know I'm eating hot dogs, drinking Miller and smoking hand-rolled Havanas with good, old George, who by the way has to laugh at all my lame jokes, if I say the right words that is.

If I feel like a skate, I phone up Bruins' GM, Harry Sinden, and say, "*Don't you think* I should be playing left wing with Oates and Neely?"

He listens and -- SHAZAM! I've got a Stanley Cup ring.

What? Oh ye of little faith. Don't forget, all I have to do is say, "Hey, Patrick Roy! *Don't you think you* should let all my shots get by you?"

He listens and -- SHAZAM! I'm a fifty-goal scorer. And that's only in one game!

Then after I've finished with self indulgence, I could turn my attention to serving my fellow man.

Using my special gift of influence I could arrange a conference call with all the world's leaders and say, "Hey, folks. *Don't you think* you should just decide to live in peace and harmony with each other and work towards the betterment of humanity?"

SHAZA . . . ! Huh?

I said, "*Don't you think* you just decide to live in peace and harmony with each other and work towards the betterment of humanity?"

SHAZA . . . ! What the . . . ?

Oh, right. I forgot. No wonder it didn't work. They're politicians. They don't listen to anyone, do they?

Justice Supreme

I have these daydreams that my Uncle Jake gets appointed to the bench. They go something like this.

After closing arguments, Justice Uncle Jake leans forward, pops a beernut into his mouth and say, "Now, let me get this straight, you want me to award your clients $20 million for the injuries they suffered because the airbags in the car they were in failed to deploy when they struck a brick wall. Have I got it so far?"

The plaintiff's lawyer starts to speak, but is silenced by Judge Uncle Jake's raised hand.

"Well, let's see," says Judge Uncle Jake, putting on his Buddy Holly glasses. "When the automobile manufacturer delivered the car to the dealer, the airbags were in working order. I guess that leaves them off the hook, right?" Justice Uncle Jake stares down at the lawyer, who nods meekly.

"And, the dealership inspected the airbags and found them to be properly installed, so that eliminates them as responsible, right?"

Again a nod.

"And while it was true the owner disconnected the airbags while making a repair, one small thing negates his liability," says Judge Uncle Jake, taking off his glasses. "The fact that he could not have anticipated your clients would steal his car!"

Justice Uncle Jake continues without missing a beat,

"You also say the insurer is responsible because the car was in an accident. However, this was no accident. Your clients drove into the side of their junior high school on purpose, while not wearing seat belts, for the thrill of bouncing off the airbags."

The lawyer buries his face in his hands.

"I find the plaintiffs responsible. Not only for their own injuries, but of a criminal act, and blatant stupidity. Therefore, I order them to pay to replace the vehicle at $23,565 and $12,368 to repair the school.

"I also find them responsible for court costs of the other parties.

"Since they are also guilty of grand theft, they are henceforth prohibited from ever owning or operating a motor vehicle. They will also be placed on home monitoring for the next three years, where I'm sure their parents will be pleased with the opportunity to get reacquainted with their darling children."

"You don't have the power to do all that!" cries their lawyer.

"Yes I do. This isn't a real courtroom. It's my nephew's daydream, so I can do anything I want. Now I order you to pay my nephew every cent you've ever earned trying to get guilty clients of the hook."

"I can't do that," protests the lawyer, "I'd be broke."

And you thought this was just fantasy.

Real T V

Have you watched any of these new reality shows on television, like *Cops* or *America's Most Wanted*? I wondered what it would be like if we had an all-reality network. Think of it. Shows that are not dramatized, but the real thing. Anything's got to be an improvement on what we've got now.

So I started thinking about some of the things that happen in the real world. The trick is to find things that are believable. There's a lot of potential. The worlds' full of reality, you know?

So here's the fall lineup of the all new reality network.

SUNDAY

20/20 Hindsight: In this new reality show couples are chosen as contestants. Each week their in-laws, who have never offered practical advice before, are allowed to criticize and second guess their adult child's decisions. This show was originally titled, *Sunday Dinner At The Folks*

MONDAY

Fifty Something: This reality drama revolves around the trials and tribulations of an average middle-aged couple, who retire early, live on their investments and split their time between a northern lake resort in summer and the Mexican coast in winter while living in a luxurious motor home that has every modern convenience.

On tonight's show Bob and Vernice wrestle with a major decision -- whether to spend November in Mazatlan or Puerto Vallarta.

TUESDAY

The Growing Pains: This Situation comedy is about a couple of neglectful parents who have to deal with their eleven teenage boys who are constantly involved in juvenile crime. This week six-foot-nine-inch, "Little Jimmy", the runt of the litter, is arrested after beating up the local sheriff's department. Oh, oh! Looks like probation for Jimmy.

WEDNESDAY

Wheel of Misfortune: On this real life game show couples take a spin at the wheel for such things as roof leaks, transmission falls out, pregnant teenage daughter and written out of Grandma's will. Watch as they go for the big one, laid off and lose the house.

THURSDAY

That's Incredulous: A show about the incredibly ridiculous things people do and think. Tonight's episode looks at individuals who think athletes are worth their enormous salaries, and a group of people in Hartford who actually paid money to see the Whalers play.

FRIDAY

The Impossible Mission: In the premiere episode a one income family tries to make ends meet on the salary of an average American worker. Watch as they try to afford such luxuries as clothes, food, and shelter. rated PG 13 (please God, I need a 13 percent raise)

SATURDAY

Red, White and Blue Dwarf: The Wacky adventure of a wealthy Texan who has never even been elected dog catcher, tries to buy his way into the White House.

I don't think that last one would work. Sure it's real. But who'd believe it.

Con-Undrum

Three buddies were fishing when it started to rain. They'd had a few beers and instead of driving decided to stay at a hotel.

"You're very fortunate," said the desk clerk, "We've had a run of soaked, drunken fishermen, so we have only one room left."

"Really?" said the first.

"Great!" said the second.

"I'll thank you to keep your, HIC! comments to yourself," slurred the third.

"Very well, said the clerk, "That will be thirty dollars."

"Okay, buck up," said the first. "Ten each." He collected the money and paid the clerk "I'll need a receipt," he said.

"Business?" asked the clerk.

"Wife," replied the first, who took the receipt and followed the other two upstairs.

A short while later the clerk discovered he'd charged the three fishermen five dollars too much. Now while it's true he was rude, arrogant, and a Toronto Blue Jays fan, he was in fact honest. A character flaw that prevented him from following his father into politics.

The rude, arrogant-yet-honest clerk rang for the bell hop.

"I've overcharged the three men in room sixteen-b. I want you to run this five dollars up to them," he said, handing him three ones and a two.

Now, the bell hop was not as rude and arrogant as the clerk. Not as honest either. And in his pragmatic, self-serving manner, he came upon a thought.

"How can three guys split five bucks evenly?" he asked himself. "Hey, they can't!" he finally answered, being somewhat slow-witted, which was the reason he hadn't followed his father into the legal profession.

After considerable thought, he said, "I'll pocket the deuce and give them back a buck each. They'll never know the difference."

So he knocked on the door, explained the situation, less the part where he lined his pockets, and gave them each a dollar.

"That's great!" said the first.

"It is?" asked the second.

"Sure, HIC!" slurred the third. "It means we only paid nine dollars each."

"Right," said the bellhop, who headed back to the front desk.

He was thinking about what happened then skidded to a stop.

"Wait a second! They only paid nine dollars each. Three nines are twenty-seven. Add the two I took and that's twenty-nine. Hey! Where's the other dollar?"

The house detective overheard the self-questioning conversation and began an investigation that eventually led to the father of the desk clerk.

How did the clerk's father end up with the missing dollar? If you'll remember from the beginning of our story, the clerk's father was in politics and a member of the current government.

Need I say more?

Politician Heal Thyself

Have you ever dreamed about the perfect job? Sure, me too.

My fantasy job pays sixty bucks an hour, I only work twenty hours a week and I don't have to do anything but watch movies and eat popcorn.

Sort of like being a union projectionist.

But what about the other side? Jobs that are a nightmare. Job's we wouldn't do no matter how much we're paid.

One day, after graduating from the communications program we were in, my buddy Shelly and I were sitting around looking at the want ads.

Neither of us had any good job prospects at the time and there weren't any in the paper.

Somehow we got onto the topic of Jobs we wouldn't want to do.

"Can you imagine being a dental hygienist?" she Asked, "spending your whole day in peoples mouths scraping stuff off their teeth."

"Yeah, think of it." I added. "Right after lunch and you get someone who's just eaten a mega-garlic caesar salad, had a few martinis, and smoked a half a pack of cigarettes."

"Now that's gross."

"I can think of a worse one though" I said.

"What's that?"

"Dental hygienist have got it easy. How'd you like to be a proctologist?"

"That's worse," said Shelly. "Definitely."

"You'd probably welcome spending all day in people mouths after spending all day in their . . . ."

"I get the picture," she said raising a hand to halt further details.

"Have you ever seen those bumper stickers? You know, 'ACCOUNTANTS HAVE BETTER FIGURES'. How about, 'PROCTOLOGISTS GET YOU IN THE END'.

"Cut it out!"

"And what if the sticker was on a BMW? Then the BMW would stand for . . . ."

"Enough already."

"Come on, Shel, if the job pays enough you'd take almost anything."

"No I wouldn't."

"Sure you would."

"You may prostitute yourself, but I won't."

"How about Public Relations Director for Exxon? That would pay major domo."

"Exxon! I'm unemployed, But I'm not a masochist."

Then I spotted an ad in the paper.

"Hey, I've got one for you, Shel," I said, focusing in on the ad. "How'd you like to be Public Relations Director for the local MP?"

"You're kidding! Wow, that would certainly be a challenge."

Shelly has a slight gift for understatement.

"Oh, hold on," I said furrowing my brow in concentration. "Oh too bad. You're not qualified."

"I've got a diploma. I'm qualified."

"No you're not. They want a medical degree too."

"And why is that?"

"Not only would you have to create a new public image for him, you'd have to treat him as well."

"Treat him! For what?"

"The guy's put his foot in his mouth so often he's developed athletes tongue."

ABOUT THE AUTHOR

Brock Macdonald

Vancouver-born Brock Macdonald is a former educator, syndicated humour columnist, and an award-winning print and TV reporter. In 2004, he left journalism to direct communications for the Recycling Council of British Columbia, and would eventually serve as its CEO for 15 years. He holds a de-gree in communications from Kwantlen College, and a master's in leadership from Royal Roads University where he was nominated for a Governor General's Gold Medal for his thesis on organizational change and governance. It was not the least bit funny.

BOOKS BY THIS AUTHOR

Faceoff Brewing

On the loose in East Vancouver, three natural-born killers. Penalty killers that is. Travis McWong, Kevin Newcombe, and Scott Wheeler are the Hastings Hurricane, a line that's played together more than two decades. Never drafted, they set Junior records for shorthanded goals, and killed penalties for Canada. Now, they've found a way into the NHL. But can these East Van rink rats save both Vancouver from a losing season, and an owner from losing the team altogether? Wherever there's a faceoff, at their craft brewery, or on the ice, the Hurricane know when to pour it on to ensure karmic justice is best served cold.

Made in United States
North Haven, CT
08 July 2022